THE HAWK, OR OTHER WORLDS
BY A.J. AARON

"What makes you think that human beings are sentient and aware? There's no evidence for it. Human beings never think for themselves, they find it too uncomfortable. For the most part, members of our species simply repeat what they are told — and become upset if they are exposed to any different view. The characteristic human trait is not awareness but conformity, and the characteristic result is religious warfare. Other animals fight for territory or food; but, uniquely in the animal kingdom, human beings fight for their "beliefs." The reason is that beliefs guide behavior, which has evolutionary importance among human beings. But at a time when our behavior may well lead us to extinction, I see no reason to assume we have any awareness at all. We are stubborn, self-destructive conformists. Any other view of our species is a self-congratulatory delusion." ~Michael Crichton, The Lost World

Written by:
Philip Turek
(3-18-15)

Other Books by A.J. Aaron:

Power, Control, Conformance
Reluctant Gods
Reluctant Gods II - The Demon Seth
Reluctant Gods III - Reset
Reluctant Gods IV - Aysel - The Prequel
Reluctant Gods - Books One Through Four
A New Reality - A Wake up Call to Life's Mysteries

Acknowledgments

Thanks to:

- My parents, Gene and Henry, for their support and faith.
- My daughter and son, Kate and Ross, for believing in me.
- My brother, Mike and his family for prodding me forward.
- My muse and sounding board, Jen.
- My friends who patiently listened to my excited explanations of my latest projects.
- My copy editor, Christine Winsor for cleaning it all up.

1

The factory resonated with production, as usual.
The warehouse overflowed with inventory, as usual.
The workers labored with their tools, as usual.
A hawk nested in the warehouse rack?

2

I spent the last three weeks drinking Pabst Blue Ribbon beer, the cheapest stuff at my local pub, and eating off the dollar menu at McDonald's so I could go out to a high-class place tonight. They say if you want to get rich, you need to hang out with rich people.

I wore my new khaki pants, ten-dollar boat loafers I picked up at the Salvation Army, and a white golf shirt that had an imitation horse logo of an expensive shirt. My supervisor dressed that way at work, so I thought I'd fit in with a better crowd dressed that way. When I entered the place, I realized how wrong I was.

The hostess was slim and pretty with shoulder-length, brown hair and wore a black dress and heels. She looked at me with pity as I walked into the restaurant and bar.

"Sir," she said.

She reached her thin fingers with short red fingernails, out to stop me. "Sorry, you need a coat and tie to go in. We have a dress code." She looked at my belly hanging over my belt.

I really needed to lose fifty or sixty pounds to drop my BMI below the obese rank.

"Uh, sorry, I didn't know. I've been saving up to come here for three weeks. I guess I should have checked first. My mistake."

I turned to leave and felt a tug on my shirt collar.

"Wait," I heard her say.

She came out from behind her little podium and pulled the tag off my collar, snapping the plastic cord. I tried to turn back around to face her.

"Don't move, sir, and excuse my touch. You have another."

She tugged at the back waistband of my pants and I heard the snap as she took off another tag.

"There, all better now. You can borrow a coat and tie if you'd like and then you can go in."

I turned back to her. She handed me the price tags. How embarrassing. "Thanks, uh, do you think it would be okay for me to do that? I mean, will I look okay?"

She smiled and looked me up and down. "I think you'll look cute. Who cares what anyone else thinks? You deserve a night out. Next time you can dress more to the accepted standard if you want, or you can realize that everyone here is just a stuffed shirt." Her light green eyes showed her sympathy and caring.

She walked down a mahogany paneled corridor and opened a small closet with several coats and ties. She picked out a brown sport coat and held it for me to wear.

I put it on. "Good choice. It fits," I said.

She handed me a beige tie with brown horses on it. "Men's room is down the hall. Once you have the tie on, you can come back and go into the bar."

"Thanks. You've been really nice. I'll be right back."

I took the tie into the men's room and put it on. I combed my mousey-brown, wind-blown hair with my fingers, and looked into the mirror. What a dork. Golf shirt with a tie, five foot ten, two hundred fifty pounds of loser.

Back out to my new friend, she smiled at me. "Not bad. Enjoy." She held her arm out pointing the way to the bar.

"Thanks. I really appreciate your help."

I walked into the L-shaped bar and sat in the back corner, against the wall. The padded leather stool with padded arms and back was comforting, being able to take the weight off my sore feet. My boss kept saying he was replacing the mats we stood on soon, but my feet didn't feel any better for the promise. I tested the chair, turning it on its swivel - it beat the hell out of the solid wood stools back in the pub by my place.

A bartender came over dressed in a black vest with a white shirt, black bowtie, with slicked back, black hair. "My name is William. May I help you, sir?"

"I'm Dave." I stuck out my sweaty hand. He shook it and then wiped his with a linen napkin. He had the composure of a priest. "Yeah. Uh, I'd like something to drink."

"What might that be? A non-alcoholic beverage or something more interesting?"

"More interesting."

"A fermented beverage or a distilled one?"

"Distilled, I think."

"Mixed, rocks, or neat?"

"I'll cut to the chase, William. How about a Manhattan? This feels like a Manhattan kind of place."

"Of course, sir. Rye, Bourbon, or Scotch?"

"Yeah. How about Jack Daniels?"

"We don't stock that, will Blanton's do? I think you'll enjoy it more than Jack."

"Sure, thanks."

The bar was about half full. By now, most of the bar was looking at me as I finally placed my order. I could have ordered a beer and simplified the process, but I wanted a Manhattan. Next time I'd ask for a Blanton Manhattan rocks.

I put ten bucks on the bar.

The bartender put my drink on a folded linen napkin.

"You can charge it if you'd like. We accept all the cards."

"No thanks. I have to use up some of this cash."

"Then it will be twelve dollars, sir."

I took another bill from my wallet and handed him the two tens.

"Thank you, sir." He turned, made change for me and placed it on the bar. I handed him a five and put the rest under my napkin.

He raised his eyebrows. "Thank you kindly, sir."

I had eight more tens in my wallet and I slid them under the napkin so I wouldn't have to keep opening my wallet for drinks. My underwear should have been as nice as that napkin was.

I looked around. Everyone reeked of money. Maybe if I tried harder in high school, and conformed to what they told me to do, a college might have accepted me and I could have been like them.

Except I had my own plan. A plan that was a lot easier. I was gonna make it with sports. I didn't need good grades, besides, that took too much effort, and if I didn't make it in sports, I'd be a rock star or own my own business and be rich. Why waste time and effort getting good grades?

I smelled my drink - toffee, leather, wood smells. I could get used to these. I tasted it and the flavors ran across my tongue - fabulous. Now, how would I network with these folks?

No one was staring at me anymore. They were all in conversation and I didn't have a clue how to start talking to them. What would I say? Hey, how do I get rich? Have any advice to give me? They'd probably tell me to learn how to dress, lose some weight, and get an education.

I downed five drinks that night. My wallet was officially empty. The bartender did well by me, though. No one talked to me except him, until I was about ready to leave.

A woman I hadn't seen that evening stood next to me. I looked up at her from my hunched-over-the-bar, drank-too-much position with droopy eyes, and smiled. She was drop dead gorgeous. Long black hair, pale skin, doll-like face with high cheekbones, pouty lips, and high-arched eyebrows – intense. Reminded me of a video game heroine. Part demon and part human. I stared at her unconsciously. She seemed familiar, yet not.

She spoke with what sounded like a Scottish accent and I swooned. "Do I know you?" she asked.

I stared, lost in her face.

"You seem so like someone I knew," she said.

"Uh, I dunno."

"Well your elocution could use some work. Maybe a better suit of clothing as well."

"Elocution?"

"The person I knew would never have used the word dunno, or got, or gonna, or ain't, as is so common amongst the lower class here. No insult intended of course, dear sir."

"Of course. What was that word again? The E one?" I grabbed a napkin and leaned over for William's pen, which he handed me.

She looked at me up and down. "Elocution." She grabbed the pen and napkin and wrote it down for me.

"Well, did you have a nice time tonight?" One eyebrow of hers rose in inquisition. Light blue eyes with black rings around the iris.

"Yup. I sure did." I smiled, and for some stupid drunken reason I took out my wallet and showed her its emptiness.

"Good. Well, have a lovely remainder of the evening. I hope I'll see you here again sometime. Look up that word for me, will you?" She turned and left. I watched her go as I held my wallet dumbly in my hands. She looked powerful and influential as she walked out the door.

I folded my wallet, but it wasn't folding right. I looked inside to see if my grocery store card had turned again. It wasn't the card keeping it from folding. It was filled with hundred dollar bills.

3

The night had started with ten, ten-dollar bills and after I spent them, I had ten, one-hundred-dollar bills. How the hell did they get in there? The only thing I could think of was the woman. Somehow, she put them in there when I was staring at her, after I showed her my empty wallet. Why would she do that and how? I had to find her.

The bartender told me he didn't know her name, but I bet he did. I even offered him a hundred and he wouldn't tell me. He did tell me what the word meant. It was how a person spoke to sound classy. He said he took elocution lessons as a child, which is why he spoke so well.

I could get a real suit and tie with the money, go back to that place, and even eat dinner. Maybe I'd see her again. She had thought she'd known me, too. Maybe we could get to know each other. As bad a night as it seemed to have been at first, it sure ended well. Beat the hell out of hanging out at the local pub drinking cheap beer with my buddies.

On the drive to work Saturday, I splurged and scarfed down two, sausage, egg, and cheese McGriddles, and a cup of java I clocked in at work with a pounding head, like just about everyone else on a Saturday morning. We only had to work a half-day, so it was bearable. The material handler, Joe, was loading parts on my conveyors for me to assemble.

"Didn't see you at the pub last night. You have a date or somethin'?"

"Nah. Just didn't feel like it. Tried a new place."

"What place? Why didn't you ask me to go?"

"It's called the Velvet Hammer."

"Shit. Too expensive for me. What'd you do? Propose to someone?"

"Just had some drinks."

"You're sick, Dave. There must be pressure on your brain or somethin'. Spending all that money down there by yourself."

Joe took off to get components for someone else and I ran my machine. My feet ached against the thin rubber mat on the cement floor. The job was pretty good, though. Made almost thirteen bucks an hour with paid benefits and time off, and I could dream and think while I did it - as long as guys like Joe didn't bug me. I made my quota most of the time, unless something broke on my machine.

I fell into the rhythm and my hands moved almost unconsciously as I thought about the weekend. I'd get off work at one and I could buy a suit and some clothes off the rack at this place downtown they advertise on TV all the time. I kept seeing the woman's face in my mind. She was like no woman I'd ever seen; yet she seemed familiar.

The buzzer announced the end of the day and I cleaned up my area, washed up, and punched out. It was the perfect day outside - about seventy degrees and sunshine. Cut grass filled my nose with its sweet scent.

I walked to the back of the lot where I parked my fourteen year old Chevy Impala, so it was the least noticeable. The paint on it looked like it had some sort of skin disease, and there were so many spots of rust, it was amazing the body stayed on. The door squealed in protest when I opened it. Shit, needed gas again - another fifty bucks. I needed a new car bad.

On the way into town, I turned up the radio and sang along to drown out the sound of my busted muffler. What sounded like a gunshot made the steering wheel jerk as the tire flapped on the cement and I pulled to the side.

I changed out the bald tire, which was brutally murdered by a piece of hubcap, with the mini-tire and limped the old warhorse into town. There it was. The same storefront on TV where the owner always stood and promised how good he'd make you look. Maybe I'd see him today and he'd give me a deal.

I walked in and the bells rang over the door. The place smelled like fabric - that chemical kind of smell they dip the stuff in at the dry cleaners. "Mind if I wash up somewhere? I had to change a flat for a little old lady." I showed the person at the cash register my filthy hands.

"What a nice guy. You deserve a deal. Sure. In the back left corner."

"Thanks."

I managed to get somewhat clean. Clean enough not to get anything dirty, that is, and I returned to the sales floor. The person from behind the register was waiting for me outside the door. He clasped his hands behind his vest. "All better?"

"Yeah. I think it'll do." I showed him my hands.

He nodded approval. " What can I do for you today?"

"Is Crazy Eddie from TV here?"

"Nope. He lives in Cancun. Has a mansion there on the beach."

"Nice. Well, I saw his advertisements and I want you to make me look good, like the commercials say." I patted my gut and laughed.

He eyed me up and down and walked around me. "We can take care of you. Suits are great for that. The belly you have will make you look more like a rich, overfed, moneymaker. It's like a trophy telling the world you have the resources for excess in life. Of course we're gonna make you look good. Any preferences?"

"Yeah, I wanna look like a young Harrison Ford."

"Uh, how about a young John Candy instead. That might be easier." He laughed. "Only kidding. Come over to the suit coats first."

9

He led the way. "Power? Wealth? Sex? Friendly? Likeable? What do you want to express?"

I stared at him and thought about what he said. I never thought a suit could say so much. His dark Latino eyes blinked as he pulled his vest down and adjusted his tie in the mirror. He continued to admire his reflection. "What's the matter? I bet you want all of it, right?"

"Yeah. All of it would be great."

He turned back to me. "I have just the thing." He took a coat off the rack and held it for me to try on. "Sixty-forty blend, fully lined back, faint red and blue pinstripes to match ties for different purposes, and a dignified, refined charcoal gray. This for an interview?"

I looked in the mirror. The coat looked stupid with my Duck Dynasty tee shirt. "Nah, just for going out to nice places."

"Well, this will work." He pulled the sleeves down and pulled the back. "I think this is your size. We can adjust the sleeves and length while you wait. Shoulders look perfect. Like it? What places do you go out to?"

"The Velvet Hammer." I looked at myself in the mirror. "I guess it'll look better with a real shirt."

"We can set you up with those, too. Shirts are forty each or four for one twenty. The Hammer, huh? All the movers and shakers go there. They all come here for their suits, too. We put an Alexander Amosu tag over the made in China tag, so they can say they have an Alexander Amosu. Yours will be the same. None of them would know an Alexander Amosu if it hit them in the face. Hundred grand a pop. Made from two weird animals called the qiviuk and the vicuna.

"Anyway, heard there's a strange woman who appears there and then leaves and no one knows anything about her. Seen her? Tall, hot accent." He led me over to the shirts and pulled out four in my size. "I assume four of them. It's a better deal."

"Four's good. I'm always dripping food on them." I showed him my tee shirt with McDonalds' drippings.

"Gotta be more careful, sir. Food will trash these." He measured my neck, arms, and waist. He dug through the shirts. "Yeah, I never saw her there. Those who have, said she's something different. 'Otherworldly', one guy said." He pulled out four in different colors.

"She spoke to me. She said she hoped to see me there again."

He stopped and looked into my eyes. "No shit."

"No shit."

"Well then we gotta make you look even better than John Candy. Let me measure you for the pants."

He took out a cloth measuring tape and had me spread my legs so he could get in there. "Got the length." He took me over to the pants and pulled out a pair with jagged bottoms. He folded the hems and handed them to me. "Here, take these and this shirt and go try them on. I'll get a belt and the vest and some ties and we can mark you up, do the alterations, and get you outta here so you can go catch that woman."

I tried on the outfit, tie and all, and looked in the three-way mirror. After the pants weren't dragging on the floor and the coat was adjusted, I looked like I was meant to wear those clothes. My sneaks didn't do them justice, though.

He tapped on them as he adjusted the hem of the pants. "Having a sale on Italian loafers."

"Yeah. I'll need them. Socks, too, now that I think of it. Grayish white socks wouldn't look good, huh?"

"Not for the goddess."

We did it. Suit fitted, all the accouterments, and even a tie tack. After gas and paying some of my debts at the plant from lost bets, I had already spent some of the money. All I had left was $737, so that's what he charged me. It was a good deal.

I had a thousand saved in checking, though, so I could hit the bank teller in Wal-Mart for some cash. I could use an ATM, except I liked having tens instead of twenties. It felt like more money.

I held the suit and bags over my shoulder. The plastic covering whispered against my tee shirt. I reached out and shook his hand. "Thanks. You made this easy."

He stuffed a card in my hand. "If you ever want something and don't want to wait, I have all your measurements. Call me and I'll have it ready for you that day. Good luck with the exotic woman. Be careful with her. I can't believe she actually talked to you."

"Yeah. Me too. Okay. Thanks."

4

On the way home I stopped at the bank in Wal-Mart, bought a fresh pack of boxers, and then got a haircut at Best Cuts. She did a real nice job and if I weren't so frickin' fat, I'd have looked pretty good.

I showed my bar napkin to a guy at the front desk of a bookstore. He found a bunch of CDs I could listen to and improve my electrocution.

At the golden arches, I purchased my favorite low calorie surf and turf - a Filet-O-Fish and a Grilled Onion and Cheddar Burger, with a small fry and a Diet Coke. It was gone in a few bites and didn't really fill me up, but I had to start my weight loss program somewhere.

I listened to the tips and tricks on the CDs during the ride home. After arriving at my domicile, I showered, shaved, put on a new pair of underwear, and laughed how my mom used to make sure I had good underwear - in case I was run over by a beer truck. Right then I heard her say, "David, you need your underwear changed." Weird.

I put on the suit and it felt foreign. Looking at my reflection, it was definitely an improvement. I hoped the woman would recognize me.

Walked over the neighbor's dog's shit on my lawn, kicked a beer bottle off the front lawn into the weed-filled flower bed, out to the car and cracked open the driver's side door. When I realized the shape my car seats were in, I knew I couldn't sit on that gunk wearing my new suit. How come I hadn't noticed it before? You needed a body condom to ride in my car and stay clean.

The sunbaked smell coming from it was worse than my high school gym locker. I earned a D in gym from skipping so much, so you'd think the locker wouldn't have smelled bad. And I took my stuff home at the end of the year for my mom to wash. She'd take a whiff and say, "Why can't you be more like your brother?"

Returning to my domicile, I noticed I needed to finish repainting it. I made sure to keep my distance from the rusty paint can and brush I'd left on the step when Joe had called me with free tickets for the game three weeks ago.

I looked through the closets for something I could keep my suit clean with and found an afghan my grandmother made in a garbage bag. She made all of us one to remember her by. Grabbed some Lysol and some Old Spice.

Back out, I covered my seat with the crocheted rose afghan, making sure to keep the tassels from getting stuck in the door. Sprayed the whole rest of the inside with Lysol, then covered my face and hands in Old Spice and tossed the bottle on the passenger seat.

Fifty miles an hour on the freeway with the car listing down on the right front from the mini-tire on there. People I passed stared at a dressed up John Candy with roses on his headrest and seats. I ignored them.

I drove past the valet since I couldn't put him through the embarrassment of dealing with my car, and parked ol' Bessie down the street. I checked the license plate. If it had fallen off, they'd tow it thinking it was abandoned. Still had a good screw on one corner and another rusted solid. I was good.

Exiting the car, I buttoned my coat and sniffed myself. I smelled mostly like new suit with a tinge of locker and some sweet spice on top. I'd be good by the time I entered the restaurant.

The same hostess was there. She did a double take when I walked in. "It's you. Look how handsome you are."

"It's me, all right. Dave. Thank you for recognizing me. I was wondering if anyone would."

She came out from behind her podium. Same black dress uniform from the other night. "Dave. I never did get your name. My name is Ellen." She poked her tiny hand at me. I shook it.

"Nice to see you again, Ellen."

"You too, Dave. So, did you come to take me to dinner? I get off in half an hour. Been here all day." She flashed her white teeth in a genuine smile as she took my new handsomeness in.

"That would be a delight. Maybe another time. I think I'm meeting someone here tonight."

Her face dropped. "Well, okay then, maybe next time." She looked nervous and embarrassed. "Dinner, the bar, or both?"

"Just the bar, thanks."

She looked at her reservation chart while she held her arm out giving me permission to enter.

The same seat I was in before was available. I unbuttoned my coat, seated myself, and William came over. "Dave, is that you, sir? You look quite dapper." He slid a folded linen napkin before me. "Your usual, sir?"

I sat up feeling proud he did that for me. I guess he remembered me. "Yes, William, thank you."

"Would you like some appetizers? It is happy hour and they are on the house. Foie gras on toast wedges, ahi tuna on cucumber slices, and my favorite, cooked ground sausage baked with cheddar on a little rye toasts. We call them sow fromage canapes."

I laughed. "That's funny, we call them shit on a shingle and have them for football snacks. Those words must have been in someone's electrocution training."

William laughed. He took a linen bar napkin and wrote the word down, then read it to me as he pointed at it. "Elocution, sir.

May I serve you the appetizers? They're around the corner and the bar isn't busy yet. All three?"

"Yes, thanks. Can I keep your note? I left the last one at the bookstore when I bought some..." I looked at the napkin. "Elocution training CDs."

"Very good, sir! I'll mix your drink first so you aren't parched." William busied himself as if he were taking care of the President or something. This was nice.

I looked around the bar. A man at the other end was staring at me. A leather-bound journal or calendar, sat in front of him. He left his book and came over, carrying a drink with no ice. He reached out a hand. I took it and felt his fat gold ring under my fingers as I gave him a good solid shake and introduced myself. "Dave."

He looked into my eyes with a question on his face. "Stan. Were you here last night?"

"Yes, I was."

"I thought so. You look different."

"Yes, I was on vacation for a while and I was slumming. However, I wanted to have some drinks. William mixes the finest."

William put my drink in front of me. "I'll fetch your appetizers, sir."

"Thanks," I said.

Stan pointed his drink at me in agreement. "Yes, he does. So you spoke to the mystery woman. She doesn't come here often and rarely speaks to anyone. Do you know her?" He leaned against the bar alongside me. Silver eyes and thick silver hair. His ring glinted under the mini-spots shining on the bar. I needed a ring like that. My mom would shit.

"No. She said we might see each other again, though. So I'm thinking I might see her tonight."

"Super. When you do, maybe you can find out what she's all about. She has everyone curious here. There isn't much we don't know about each other. It's more like a country club than a restaurant."

"I'll do that."

"So Dave, what do you do? I never saw you here before. You were on vacation, huh? Must be nice to be able to take time off, let go, and just hang out."

"Yeah, love doing that. Traveling for vacation can be more work than it's worth." I sipped my drink and hoped he didn't ask me what I did again.

"So, what did you say you did?" He felt my suit. "Nice suit."

I showed him the tag on the inside pocket.

"Ah, same as mine." He showed me his tag and smiled. "Amosu has the finest fabrics, don't you think? Worth every cent."

"Sure are." I nodded, thinking I evaded the question again.

"What did you say you do?"

"Uh, I didn't. I can't really talk about it."

Stan's eyes opened wide and he stood up nodding. He held his drink out to clink mine. "Say no more, old man. I had you pegged for CIA - the FBI guys are thinner. CIA is better paid, and with a suit like that, you're doing well. I'm a judge and I know plenty about the folks in this town. If you need any help, you let me know. Stan Seymour is my name." He shook my hand again.

"Thanks, I appreciate that."

"Well, I'll let you go. You're probably on some clandestine mission, so I don't want to interfere. Besides, my wife's here chatting with her cackling friends at the table already. I just wanted a quiet moment to sip my drink before I had to listen to them all through dinner. Nice to meet you."

"You too, Judge Seymour."

"No, Stan, please call me Stan."

"Okay, Stan. Nice to meet you, too."

Stan returned to his seat and picked up his book. William went to him. Stan whispered in his ear and left.

William came back with a plate of appetizers for me. "Here you are, sir. Something to fuel your body for your next mission."

"Mission?"

William looked around the bar and leaned into me. "Don't worry, sir. Your secret is safe with me. Judge Seymour told me you were on a clandestine CIA mission. Something about the mystery woman. The electrocution thing and the way you spoke the first night were good covers, but you need not bother with such window dressing for me. Your secret is safe, sir."

"Uh, there is no——"

William motioned to zip his lips. "Loose lips sink ships. I know. If you tell me, you'd have to kill me. Say no more. I will have to use the appellation, Sir David from now on to recognize the knight in shining armor you really are." He smiled proudly.

"Well, I suppose if that makes you feel better, you can call me that."

Heck, why not? Sir David sounded pretty classy.

"May I get you some water with lemon, Sir David? Maybe some wine for the appetizers?"

"Uh, yes. That would be nice."

William took off to polish a glass and pour my wine. I hardly ever drank wine and I never remembered what brand I liked when I went to buy it.

He came back with two different glasses, one red, and one white. He told me what they were, though I didn't pay much attention. They tasted good with the snacks. The fogra on toast wedges were great. It looked like it came out of one of those squirt cheese cans. Pretty fancy.

William came back. "Another plate, sir? I see you could use another drink as well. May I?" He held my glass and waited.

"Sure. Why not? Hey, the fogra stuff on toast - does that come in a squirt can? I'd like to buy some."

"I'm glad you're fond of it. Not a can. That came out of a pastry decorator. It's a blend of goose and duck liver with fat and seasonings. As I said, sir, you can drop the act when it is only I with you. Fogra. Comical."

"Liver?"

"Yes, sir."

"Uh, better skip that one on the next round."

"Very good. You are a man of discipline. Denying yourself your favorite food to watch your cholesterol."

"Yes, cholesterol of course." As if I ever gave a crap about cholesterol. The thought of eating liver is just gross. I didn't care how good it tasted.

He promptly replaced my drink and set off to do the rest. I sipped and looked around. The marble of the bar glistened. I don't know how I missed her entry, yet the woman appeared right next to me. I realized it when I heard her seductive, accented voice in my ear.

"Hello, David. Glad to see you. Things will be better soon, dear." She sat in the seat next to me. I looked at her face, absorbed by it. She looked as good as when I was drunk. You never know. Sometimes you see 'em sober and wonder what zoo you found them at. I stared.

She smiled. Her foreign-looking face matched her foreign-sounding speech. "I see you've invested in yourself. That's good. I was hoping you had a taste for the finer things in life. It will make things easier for us."

"Us? Uh, sure. Shall we go into the restaurant? I've started listening to elocution CDs. I believe it has already had an impact on my presentation. Please give me the pleasure of dining with you, and I will be forever in your debt. How's that?"

She laughed a little. "Good for you. "We may someday dine, not tonight, though." She gave me a flat-lipped smile that raised her already high cheekbones and arched an eyebrow. "We may have a relationship should you continue to show promise. I'd like you to do a simple job for me. A series of jobs, in fact."

"Sure. What jobs?"

"I'd like you to make deliveries to high-ranking people in society. Influential, important people. In addition, each time you do, I'll pay you one thousand dollars. You must do it before five, since most white collar workers are gone from their offices by then. Moreover, you must dress in a manner as you have tonight, conforming to accepted standards, use proper elocution, and present yourself confidently. Are you interested?"

"A thousand a delivery?'

"Yes."

"What is it?"

"Merely a small package about a dollar bill's length on each side."

"What's in it?"

"Something different each time."

"Drugs? A bomb?"

"Of course not. Nothing illegal or dangerous at all. It is very important each package be delivered though, as they are quite precious."

I looked into her exotic eyes to try to see if she was lying. I never did very well determining that. Cost me buying a used car with a transmission just good enough to drain a tank of gas in it before it broke, along with a bunch of other things I fell for over the years. Like having my own business selling soap - what a scam. I had to try this, but I wanted to feel good about it.

I watched her closely and said, "Not illegal, no drugs or bombs. That's a chunk of change for delivering a package."

"Yes, very special deliveries. They must occur in the time allotted of two hours by a professional-looking gentleman. It's worth the price for these customers. Will you do it for me, David?" She never flinched and kept eye contact the whole time - not lying. I was lost in her eyes and face again.

"David?"

"Uh. Sure. Why not?"

"Good. Give me your cell phone number."

I flipped my little phone open.

"Nice phone," she said as she laughed.

Who remembers their own number? No one ever calls themselves. I looked it up - showed it to her.

She nodded. "I will store it under the name of my ex-mate. You will now be known as Argus. When I text you, you can enter my name as Ekaterina."

"Code names, huh? Neat."

"Yes. I suppose you could say it's a code name."

"Ekaterina, sounds Russian or something?"

"Yes, it does. I will pay you as before. It should already be there as another bonus for agreeing to our arrangement. Goodnight."

I reached into my pocket and took out my wallet. When I looked back up, she was gone. My wallet was stuffed with hundred dollar bills again.

5

Sunday I drove to NTB and had them replace my flat with their cheapest tire. They said I needed almost four grand worth of work after their free inspection - brakes, alignment, system flushes, brake lines, and on and on. I told them I only used it to drive around my estate.

One hour and two cans of Lysol spray later, the car was emptied out and all the trash thrown away along with some moldy beef jerky and a rotten apple. I parked it in the sun with the windows down; trying to kill whatever else was left inside.

I walked to the pub to watch the game with the guys. I knew I was doing the right thing after listening to their chatter, smelling the pub, and feeling how uncomfortable those darn stools were compared to the Velvet Hammer's. After six beers and three beer dogs, I left before the game was over.

I walked home and rolled up my car windows. It was still light out and I thought I should burn off the beer and dogs. I looked at the dog shit on the grass. Most of it was starting to turn white; it had been there so long. The grass looked like it could use a trim, but the way it waved in the breeze; I didn't want to mess with it.

My neighbor with the offending dog came out on his front porch. "Hey, shithead. When you gonna mow your grass?" he yelled, while his pit bull tugged against its leash, snarling.

I stood tall and countered him brilliantly. "Why, so your mutt can see over it when he drops his feces on my grass? Go fornicate."

He turned red. "It's a she, not a he, and she's a purebred that would bite your head off if I wanted her to. And yeah, she can't see over the grass when she shits on it. Since when do you talk so high class? Look at your yard and look at mine. Which one do you think is more suitable for a toilet?"

I looked at them both as if I was evaluating his comment. "Your yard looks like a sissy owns it. Pretty mirrored ball and pink flamingo there, Elvis. I wouldn't defecate there either, even if I were a girl." I turned and entered my domicile. The wooden screen door slammed behind me to punctuate my statement.

I decided to skip the yard work. My living room smelled somewhat like the car, just a little less sweet. I decided to fill up as many trash bags as I needed to, since I purchased a bunch the other day for a special occasion like this. Heck, if things worked out with this delivery job, I might want to have a lady-friend come visit. Maybe the hostess at the Velvet Hammer.

I removed pizza boxes off the recliner so I could sit and better analyze the situation. I fell asleep.

After hearing some muttering, scuffling, and someone chuckling on my front porch, I woke up. By the time I looked out, whoever it was had left and there was a fresh pile of shit right on my welcome mat.

Looking at my watch, I had an hour to get cleaned up and get to work. Plenty of time.

I managed to not step in the poop on the way out. Bessie smelled better, but she still had some evil stuff going on in her and I was glad when I finally made it to work.

I was assigned my favorite machine, the one I always beat rate on because it's set up the best for the least amount of movement to assemble the parts. I wondered when Ekaterina would contact me. How many packages would she want me to deliver? Would it turn into a full-time job?

Doing the math in my head - five days a week less holidays, since I doubted any office folks worked Saturdays or holidays for the most part. Once a day would be...holy shit, I mean feces. That would be a dream. I could quit my job on one package a day! Over two hundred grand a year. Screw cleaning up the house and car. I'd just get new ones.

My phone vibrated in my pocket. I checked my count and looked at the time on the wall clock. I was good. Even though we can't use our phones when we're working, they don't ride you so much if you're ahead.

I took it out. It was a text from a number I didn't know. It said, "Ekaterina here. Pick-up will be ready by three and must be delivered no later than five. Hopefully they're still there at five, so sooner is better." She gave the address for the pick-up and drop-off, along with the customer's name.

It was two-thirty. I had to go home, change, drive to the pick-up, then to the drop-off. If I left now, I'd be there by four. I could do it. I texted that I was on my way.

I shut off my machine and looked for my supervisor. He was covered in grease up to his elbows working on a machine. Not good timing. I wiped my hands on my rag and walked up to him.

I tapped him on the shoulder. "Uh, Dalibor, I need to leave."

He turned and looked at me. "No."

"But I have to go. It's really important."

He stared at me with a wrench in his hand. "What? They having a sale on cheese puffs? Go punch out. Get the fuck out of here."

"Thanks. I really appreciate it."

I was home in record time since there wasn't any traffic yet. I stepped into the shower, rinsed off, and scrubbed my hands clean. I put on my suit with a new shirt and tie. I grabbed my grandma's afghan and tossed it across my seat. I drove to the pick-up point.

It was an empty field outside of the city. There were no cars, just a person standing in the middle of a field with a wrapped and decorated package. I ran over and he held it tightly to his chest and asked my name.

"Uh, Dave."

"Sorry, wrong name." He turned as if to go.

"Wait! Wait. Orgus, Urgus, Argus…that's it, Argus."

He turned back. "Good. Take it." He held it out. "Don't dawdle. Get it there on time."

I smelled it and he yelled, "No smelling, licking, or shaking. It isn't a Christmas present. Now take it and go."

I ran it back to my car and pulled away. I checked my watch. I was good. Getting across town by four o'clock should be no problem.

On the freeway back into the city. It was nice not having to drive fifty anymore since I replaced the mini-spare tire. People still stared at me, though. Guess it was the way the driver's side front fender fluttered when I made it to sixty-five.

I entered the city center and was halfway there. At a light, Bessie started to blow a little smoke from the hood. Wonder when she took that up? The next light it was a little more smoke and by the time I was through six lights, she was hissing steam like a dragon and the check engine light was on. I couldn't stop now.

A few more blocks and Bessie made a God-awful sound, like a charcoal grill smashing on the ground, and then she was completely silent.

Attempts at restarting failed, she wouldn't even turn over. She was all seized up. Bessie had passed. I checked my watch. I couldn't walk there in time, it was too far. Horns started honking. I put on my flashers and got out. A couple of guys came over and set themselves up to push her. "Hey, it's John Candy! Okay, hotshot, put it in neutral and steer her to the parking meters on the side. We'll push."

I hopped in and they pushed me to the side and left.

There was a map for the subway routes by the turnstile. I found the one I needed, bought a handful of tokens, and passed through. The subway car stunk. A bum was eating an egg salad sandwich like it was a gourmet meal and he stared at me while he chewed. He scanned me from my head to my toes and back again.

He licked his lips with a brown tongue and blinked his cloudy eyes a few times. "Spare a few bucks for a fellow traveler? They say you get back three times what you give." He wiped some drool off his chin with his cuff.

This is why I hated taking public transit. What the heck. I would make a grand today anyway. I took out my wallet and gave him a ten.

"Thank you, sir." He smiled a missing-tooth smile.

"You're welcome. Have a good day."

We sat in silence as he inspected my ten then took out a roll of money and wrapped my ten around it.

They announced my stop on the speakers and the wheels squealed as they made the turn into the station. The doors popped open and I bolted off the subway and up the stairs.

I got, uh, obtained, my bearings and headed to the drop point. I checked my phone while I walked to make sure I had the right address. A couple more blocks and I'd be there.

The heat of the day demanded I loosen my tie. People didn't notice me in the suit since everyone else was wearing one, too. I was invisible by dressing like them.

The address took me to an old high-rise office building - the Federal Building. Inside, I checked the directory. Sixteenth floor, the Department of Internal Affairs and my delivery was for the manager.

I stood before several metal detectors and an x-ray machine. What if they found something in the box? I'd probably go to jail. She wouldn't send me here knowing I'd get caught, though. Would she? I stood staring. A guard yelled at me. "Hey, if you're coming in, empty your pockets in the pan, put the package on the belt, and walk through. It's time for my break."

I looked at him. I had to stay calm so he wouldn't get suspicious and open the package.

"Of course. Good afternoon. How are you, Officer?" I emptied my pockets, put the box on the belt, and walked through. No beeps. The conveyor belt stopped. He looked closer at his screen, which I couldn't see from where I was. He looked back at me and then back at the screen.

He put rubber gloves on and picked up the box. With a pair of tongs, he picked up a small square of cloth and wiped the box with it then put the square into a machine. He smiled at me. "Explosives check." He pointed at the machine. "Just a second more."

A green light flashed on the machine. He handed me the package. "Good to go."

Well, it wasn't a bomb. And whatever he saw inside must not have been a big deal, so I was more at ease about what I was doing.

I rode the elevator up and entered the office through a glass door. A clerk stamping papers was at the counter. She looked up. "May I help you, sir?"

"Yes, I have a package for Mr. Ralph Hampton. Is he here? I have to deliver it personally."

She looked me up and down. "Who is it from?"

"Sorry, I just deliver them."

"Pretty dressed up for a courier."

"Yes. We're a very exclusive service. We maintain the highest standards. Whoever is having this delivered is impeccable."

She smirked and waved for me to follow her. She led me to an office where Ralph sat behind a desk feverishly working on a computer. She left and he looked up. "Yeah? Who are you?" His eyes blinked rapidly, one eyebrow raised. He picked up a pen and tapped it on his desk while one side of his cheek twitched.

"I have a delivery for you." I put the package on his desk.

He looked at it, as he twitched again. "Nice wrapping. What is it?"

"I don't know, sir. Maybe you should open it."

He picked it up and held it in his hands. I couldn't wait to see what was inside. He seemed mesmerized and didn't move. His cheek spasmed in little flicks.

He pulled the black satin ribbon loose. He unfolded the shiny gold paper and lifted the lid. His eyes opened wide as he reached inside and touched what was there. No more twitching. His face and shoulders relaxed. He seemed to be touching whatever was inside the box. I moved closer. He looked up at me and closed the lid. "Thank you. I'll get to it in a moment. I appreciate your promptness and will put in a good word for you to your boss."

"Thanks."

"You can go now," he said.

"Okay. Thanks."

I left the building never knowing what I delivered. How could he tell my boss I did a good job? There wasn't anything on the package that said where it came from, or who the delivery service was. Maybe it had been inside. Who cared? I had a thousand bucks coming.

6

A subway ride back to my car and I grabbed my grandma's afghan, folded it up and tucked it under my arm. I pocketed the elocution CDs I'd listened to three times already. I bent the license plates back a forth a few times, and they came right off. I ran down the street and tossed the plates in a can. Poor Bessie.

It was almost five o'clock and my stomach was grumbling. I wasn't too far from the Hammer, so I thought I'd try to get there for happy hour and have some appetizers for dinner.

The hostess saw me come in and averted her lovely light green eyes to the podium. She brushed her long brown hair to the side and behind her ear.

"Hi. How are you, Ellen?" I said.

She looked up and gave me a nervous smile. "Meeting someone, sir?"

"Dave. My name's Dave."

"Of course. Sorry, Dave. Meeting someone?"

"I'm not sure."

She looked down at the reservation sheet and held her arm out to the bar for me to go in. Guess I'm not making many points with her. She must have still been angry from when I met Ekaterina last time, rather than having dinner with her.

William beamed as I took my regular seat in the back corner at the bar. "Sir David. The usual?"

"Yes, please."

"Appetizers?"

"By all means, William. Thank you."

William busied himself preparing my drink and food. Stan waved from the other end of the bar. "Hi, Dave. See you survived the day. Always a good thing for a fellow like you."

"You're right. Only had one death today."

Stan's eyes widened and he was promptly at my side. "Can you tell me about it? Were you in any danger?"

"Well I almost missed a very important meeting because of it, not much danger, though. My partner died the way she would have wanted to. Working."

Stan looked understanding as he squinted his silver eyes at me. "Must be tough losing partners like that. Gosh. I'm so sorry for you."

"You do get attached." I looked down feigning grief.

He patted my shoulder. "Yeah. If I go, I'd like to go at my bench. It's where I feel most comfortable. Glad to see you're safe and keeping us safe. Let me buy you a drink."

"That's okay, I can't stay long. But thanks for offering."

"Of course. No rest for the weary. I have to leave myself. The wife is having her friends over and she wants me to bring home takeout. How boring that must sound to you."

"It doesn't. It sounds like it would be nice to go home to a wife and friends."

"My apologies. I bet it would. Well, have a nice evening and stay safe."

William dropped off my drink, two different wines, and the appetizers. I could get used to this. I sniffed the drink and slugged down half. When I looked up, she was sitting next to me.

"Argus. *You're making headway. Congratulations.*"

"Ekaterina. Hi. Where did you come from? How do you do that all the time?" She wore a beige silk pantsuit that may have been sexier than the dress she wore the other night. I stared into her intense blue eyes and was once again lost in her.

"Argus. You need not worry about how I get here, or where I come from. You only need to worry about getting your deliveries made."

"How often will I have them?"

"How often do you want them? We have quite a backlog right now. That's why I hired you."

I heard, *"David, you have to try your best,"* but she hadn't said it.

William came over to us. "May I get you a drink or an appetizer, my lady?"

"I'm not staying. I just need a moment with this gentlemen."

"As you like." William winked at me.

Ekaterina turned back to me. "I can give you four or five per day if you like."

I stared at her thinking. She was so darn gorgeous. Four or five per day. Let's see, four a day, five days a week, fifty weeks a year with two weeks vacation, is a million bucks. Holy shit. Guess I needed to quit my day job and do this full-time.

"Argus." She touched the back of my hand with hers. It didn't feel like skin. It felt like silk. I looked at it. It was so smooth I couldn't even see her pores. No veins, no hair. Flawless. She wrapped her fingers around my hand and squeezed it while she leaned in to my face. Her breath was on my lips. *"David. Hear me."* It smelled sweet.

"Uh, shall we dine together this evening? I have a few questions to ask."

"No dinner. Ask away."

"Well, the package made it through the federal building security easily, so I thought it was safe."

"See. No drugs or bombs."

"Yes. I mean they x-rayed it and everything. I was afraid they'd open it."

"Never let anyone except the customer open it. Understand? Do whatever you need to do to stop that from happening should it look inevitable. Anything."

"Why?"

I watched her lips form the words with her delicious accent. "It is meant for the customer and the customer only. Don't worry. If someone were to look at it, it would be okay, since it isn't anything bad and is quite innocuous and appears benign. Nonetheless, never let it get that far. They can never touch it, or they could ruin it. Understood? It is imperative you pay attention to this, or we will have a mess to clean up."

She leaned back in her seat and swung her long black hair over her shoulder. It glistened under the mini-spots in the ceiling. She waited patiently, her unblinking, piercing blue eyes fixed on mine. I must have been stuck again because she reached out and pushed my hair to the side of my forehead. "Argus. Is there anything else?"

"Sorry. My car died. I need to replace it before I start deliveries again. I'll have to save up money and shop for one. It could be a while."

Ekaterina opened her purse and took out a smart phone. I didn't recognize the brand. She held it in front of her and rather than touching the screen, she moved two fingers a few inches from the screen while the light flickered and shone on her in different colors. When she finished, she put the phone back into her beige satin purse and looked at me. "No problem."

"Sure it's a problem. I'll have to save some money up and buy a new one. That will take me some time. I can't be using public transit to do four deliveries a day."

"By the time you're done here tonight, you'll have a new car. I can't risk you doing deliveries without adequate transportation. When you leave, see the valet and he'll bring your new car around. It's black. I think you'll like it. Very fitting for a proper gentleman. Now, is there anything else?"

"Wow. It isn't stolen, is it?"

"No. The title will be in the glove box and it will have your legal name on it. Shall you start tomorrow morning, or do you need some time to wrap things up at your present employer?"

"I think I can start the day after tomorrow, Wednesday. I need to clean out my locker and let them know I quit."

"Very well then. Expect a text Wednesday morning at eight. Five a day?"

"Let's do four, if that's okay."

"Four is okay, however five is more in your pocket. Are you sure?"

"I'm not sure what I'm going to do with all of this money anyway. I think four is enough. I'll want time to eat lunch every day, too."

"Four it is. Eat light lunches though, okay? You want to be able to fit into your car. You could lose a few pounds." She stood and shook my hand with her silky flesh. "To a prosperous relationship."

She turned and walked out.

William was right there when she left. "Everything okay, Sir David? You haven't touched your food."

"Everything is fantastic."

"If you don't mind my saying so, it appears that woman has some affection for you the way she moved your hair from your face and held your hand. You are a lucky man."

"No affection, just business."

"Ah, I see, sir. Part of the cover." William looked around. He looked back at me and zipped his lips.

7

My wallet was filled again and I tipped William excessively. I was too excited to see what car she left me and I quickly finished eating. I hurried out to the valet. His eyes lit up as I approached and he located the key. He held it up. "She said she was borrowing your car when she dropped it off and to look for you. You're Dave, correct sir?"

"Uh, yes."

"You do look a bit like John Candy. I'll be right back."

He took off and ran down the street. In a minute, he pulled up in a little black thing with four interlocking rings as a hood emblem. It was blacker than black with dark windows. The engine rumbled quietly as he opened the door and held it for me.

"I think this is my all-time favorite car, sir. I see you have all the options as well. Five hundred and fifty horsepower V10, Bang and Olufsen stereo system. If you ever need to have it exercised, let me know." He smiled as his gloved hand held the door for me.

I handed him a tip. "Thanks."

My hands shook as I sat and tried to get familiar with it quickly. I adjusted the tight fitting seat to give me some more legroom. I could lose a few pounds. My feet banged into the pedals - only two, thank God. I had an automatic. I put it in gear and touched the gas. The tires screeched and it shot to the end of the drive. I jammed on the brakes. Oops. A little more responsive than Bessie was. How could it be mine when I couldn't even afford the insurance? Well, maybe I could now. I couldn't believe she'd given it to me. I should marry her.

I had to get it on the freeway. Luckily, traffic was light and I could push it. I hit the entrance ramp and gunned it. All four wheels screamed and I had to hit the brakes to merge. I was going one-ten before I hit the freeway. Yikes!

Back down to five above the speed limit and I cruised in the middle lane. The leather interior smelled rich - quite a contrast to Bessie. The suspension was rough going over the bridge because it was a sports car, not a bouncing betty like Bessie.

I exited and took the side streets home. When I looked at it parked in my driveway, I wasn't sure if it would be there in the morning. I hoped it wouldn't be stolen.

The title with my name on it was in the glove box along with a card saying I had insurance for the next year. I took the driver's manual and the title out, pushed the lock button on the key fob and the lights flashed and it beeped. At least it had some kind of security system.

Remembering the dog feces on the welcome mat, I stepped over them into my house.

The manual filled me in on all the high-tech gadgets and special maintenance of the R8 while I drank Pabst. I thought about downing a bag of Cheetos, then thought again about fitting into my new car. I fell asleep on the recliner.

When I woke, the sun was up. I startled and started to worry about being late for work, but remembered I was quitting. I had two bowls of Captain Crunch and a cup of eye-opener thinking about the whole thing. I was lucky.

I showered and put on my suit. I had to remember to call and get another suit and some shirts. I sent myself a text message for later. I opened my front door. The car was still there.

I locked the house, stepped over the dog shit, and my new best friend beeped as I unlocked her. What would I call her? R8. Hmm. Arry? Yeah. Arry.

I slid into Arry and readjusted everything. I checked out the GPS and sound system and familiarized myself with the controls. I didn't know how I could ever be late for a delivery now.

For some reason I heard my mom say, *"David, you must try. You have so much to look forward to."* Weird.

Arry gleamed where I parked in my usual spot in the back of the lot. I walked through the employee entrance and Joe was passing by on his forklift. "Hey, someone sleep over last night? I saw a hot car in your driveway this morning. And why are you all dressed up?"

"I'm starting a new job. The car is for work."

Joe jumped off the forklift. "What the fuck?" He felt my suit-coat and I pushed his hand off. "Dave, what kind of job did you get? Is it legal?"

"Yeah it is. Hey, there's Dalibor. I need to talk to him. Catch ya later."

"Okay, Dave. Catch ya at the pub."

"Yeah."

I yelled to my boss. "Dalibor! Can I speak with you?"

He stopped. "What, you going to a funeral now? Just go."

"No. I'm quitting. I have a new job."

He walked over, felt my suit-coat, and I brushed his hand away. "Who would hire you? A drug dealer?"

"No. It's legal and I start tomorrow. Just wanted to let you know. It's been great here. I have to clean out my locker."

He looked at me with a raised eyebrow. "You sure you want to do this?"

"I have to. It's a no-brainer. You'd do it, too, if you were me."

"Well don't get yourself killed. And if you need the job back, I'll take you anytime. You've been good." He stuck his hand out.

I shook it. "Thanks. You have too."

Dalibor trotted off and I cleaned out my locker. I threw everything away except pictures of us all at my mom's at Christmas wearing goofy hats my brother got us to wear every year. Cowboy hats, knit caps, little Jewish caps, cone head caps, dunce caps, and on and on. The pictures made me laugh when I needed a lift at work. I carried them out and put them in the glove compartment of my new R8 workplace.

Okay. The worst part of the day was done. Now what? I didn't have enough money to look for a new place to live yet. Tomorrow I'd make enough. I should get another suit, at least. Then afterwards, I could eat at the Hammer tonight. Maybe Ellen would eat with me.

It was only ten in the morning and the Hammer wouldn't be open yet. I drove to the Waffle House, had breakfast, drove to the suit store, and ordered a suit to pick up later.

8

With the new suit behind my seat, I pulled up to the Hammer at the time Ellen said she'd be getting off work. The valet came up smiling and opened my door. "Hello, Dave."

"Hi, uh, sorry, I never caught your name."

"It's Ralph, sir."

I exited the car. "Ralph. I won't be long. Just picking Ellen up."

"Oh, are you related, sir?"

"No. Just taking her to dinner."

"Ah, I see. Yes sir. Go ahead and I'll keep the car to the side here." He pointed his gloved hand.

"Thanks."

Ellen was excitedly gathering her things as I approached her podium. She looked up. "Very prompt. I'll just be a second."

She picked up two grocery bags with her work clothes in them. She wore a short flowered dress, with flowered high-heels, and a flowered purse to match. Her shiny brown hair was down around her shoulders and she looked lovely. It was such a contrast from her normal, black, conservative hostess-attire of the restaurant.

She smiled up at me. "May I?"

"Huh?"

She pecked me on the cheek. "I hope that wasn't too forward. It's just that I'm so excited - us going to dinner together finally. I thought you were after that mystery lady before. Maybe you still are. Are we going to the Topper?"

I laughed, enjoying her excitement. "Yup. The Topper it is. We can have drinks and look out across the city as it turns. I always wanted to go there. The mystery lady is a business acquaintance."

"I hope so. She seems scary. I've always wanted to go to the Topper, too. I can't wait," she said as she took my arm in hers.

"Let's go."

Ralph handed me the key and he held the door for Ellen. Ralph said to her, "Have a lovely evening, miss."

"I'm sure I will. Thanks."

He closed the door and we drove across town. Ellen was like a kid in a candy store looking at and touching everything in the car. "Is this new? It smells brand new."

"Yes. It was delivered yesterday. Like it?"

"Sure do. So what do you do Dave? When I first saw you I thought you had to save up in order to just have a night at the Hammer. Then William told me you were with the CIA and had some kind of top-secret assignments - like a James Bond. This car seems like it would be a James Bond car. So all that other stuff was just a cover, huh? Don't worry. Your secret is safe with me James Bond."

I looked around the car and tried to make believe I was paying real close attention to driving so I could buy some time answering her. I hit a red light. Shit. What should I tell her? I fumbled with the sound system. I couldn't lie to her about being CIA. I'm not that smart a guy. Let the others think what they want. If Ellen and I were going to date, though, she needed to know the truth.

I looked at her. "Sorry, so many distractions." The car behind me honked the horn for the green light in front of me. I drove on. "Yes. It's hard to explain. I didn't lie to you when I told you I had to save up to go to the Hammer. I did back then. It wasn't a cover."

Ellen's legs were crossed and newly manicured, long-nailed hands rested on her knees. Her eyes considered me. "Back then wasn't that long ago. Seems you've come into some good fortune. Does it have anything to do with meeting the mystery woman at the Hammer?"

"Yes, she's given me a job and this is my car now. She said she needed something more reliable for me than my old beater."

"Must be an important job. This costs more than most people's houses."

"I guess. I've worked for her once so far. Now I'll be full-time. Tomorrow is my first real day."

"So what will you be doing?"

"Uh, it's a customer service job with high class customers."

"It is? Sounds fun. Is it real estate?"

"No, not real estate. Oh look, we're here." I pulled up to the valet. He opened her door and I walked around to him. He handed me a ticket and bowed his head, then trotted around the car and took Arry away.

Ellen took my arm and we started in. "So, not real estate. Is it legal? Of course, it must be. You seem like such a nice guy."

"Yes. It's legal. Can we just enjoy the night? I don't know too much about the job yet."

"Of course. Let's have a nice celebration dinner for you."

9

The night ended well. Ellen stuck to her word and didn't ask any more questions. For a while there, it felt like the third degree my family always gave me about things. I had to figure out something to tell her, or it would not end.

I woke at six and had a light breakfast. Did my pick-ups and deliveries flawlessly and stopped by the Hammer.

Ekaterina was as strangely beautiful as ever. Tonight she wore a black leather skirt-suit tightly fitted with the skirt down to just below her knee.

"Argus, good to see you," she breathed in my ear.

I whispered back in her ear, "Don't call me Argus in here. To them I'm Dave."

"Don't worry. They won't hear. You just look so much like my old mate, much heavier of course...you should lose some weight though, dear. You'd be so much more handsome."

I pulled back from her grasp and she stood, slid her barstool closer to me, reseated herself, and slid her leg along mine. What the hell was she up to? Did she think she could just buy me like she did my car?

I looked at her. "Should we have dinner?"

"Oh no. Business only. Which, by the way, if you're doing four a day, I need to use another method for your payment. Perhaps I should leave it in the glove box of your new car at the end of the day?"

"How can you do that? Can't you just generate a check, or deposit it in the bank electronically?"

"The same way I've gotten it into your wallet each time of course. And I can't deposit it. Our business is always transacted in cash so our customers retain their anonymity."

"Anonymity?"

"Yes dear, anonymity. They would like to remain anonymous."

"I see. Charity givers. Nice."

"Why not, sure, charity givers. Philanthropists of a sort, yes."

"Okay, so cash only. You slipped it into my wallet somehow like a pickpocket would. Arry is locked and has a security system though."

"Arry?"

"Yes, I named her Arry."

"How cute. You're so much like my last mate. He was like that sometimes."

"Uh, so how will you get it into the car? You need to have a key to it. Hey, come to think of it, I didn't get a spare key with it. You must have it."

"Well, there ya go then. You're so cute and smart.

She looked and me and waited. Her lips didn't move, and still I heard her say, *"David, just think if you worked harder in school before. Now you have a chance. Don't pass it up. Come to your senses."*

"What? What did you say? Work hard?"

"I didn't say anything. Working hard is good, though. Anyway, look for the payment in your glove box. It will be there tonight when you leave. Oh, and the way things are here, you'll need to figure out how to handle all the cash. You can't just put it in the bank every day. The tax system here will be all over you. You need to, how do they say it here, wash it?"

"Wash the money?"

"Yes. What's the proper term? Laundry."

"I need to launder the money?"

"Of course. Pass the cash through a business so you can pay taxes on it. Make believe you sold, or gave a service, and received cash for it. A video store, or car wash, or something that moves a lot of cash through it."

"Shit. I never thought about that."

"That's okay. That's why I'm your teacher. Just like I was with my other Argus."

"Teacher?"

"Yes. Someone of a higher skill and ability."

She looked at her watch "Well, David. Time to go. I won't be seeing you as often from now on, but you will get paid daily. Do have a good evening." She kissed my cheek. My eyes closed. Her lips felt like silk. An exotic smell came from her skin. I opened my eyes and she was gone.

I came to my senses. This was a setback. How would I launder money? I'd have to save up, buy a business with a lump of cash. Who would do that? I'd have to store all that cash. I needed an accountant or a lawyer that could help me with this stuff - someone not quite drawing inside the lines and still legal on the books.

"Hello!" A firm slap hit me on the shoulder. Stan smiled and held his hand out.

I shook it. "Hello, Judge. Good to see you. How are things?"

"Ah, you know. Get through the day and enjoy the time after. I'm ready to retire. I just can't get used to the thought of spending every moment with the wife, even if she is the angel she is." He sat in the seat next to me.

I thought maybe Stan could find someone to help me. I patted his shoulder. "Tough stuff. I see your point, but the job must give you some pleasure, too, doesn't it? I mean, seeing all those criminals getting what they deserve."

Stan waved his glass at William who quickly came for it. "Yes. It does. Something I'm sure we both have in common." He looked around the room to see if anyone was watching. "I'm sure you'd understand not being able to catch some of the worst culprits out there having the job you have. Try as our legal system does, it can't catch all of them and sometimes we end up giving them more freedom by obtaining evidence the wrong way."

William dropped off a fresh drink for Stan. "Sir David. May I get you anything else?"

"I'm good." William refreshed my water and neatened up my area while I continued. "Yes, of course Stan. We've had our share of those. I think the worst are the ones that help the true criminals launder money and look legit."

Stan's eyes lit up and he clunked his glass on the bar as he put his hand on my shoulder and looked into my eyes. "Damn right. Those damn accountants and lawyers that set these guys up. Perfectly legal and legit. Would love to catch them doing something wrong."

"Sure would. Anyone I should know about? Professionally that is. Could be a threat, or could lead to others that are."

"Of course. Why didn't I think of that? We need to share information. Nothing illegal about that. The biggest and most successful one out there does big and small businesses. We had bugs on him. Unfortunately, never with a court order, since we couldn't come up with due cause, and so what we found was useless. He caught us and we can't bug him anymore." Stan nodded and sipped his drink.

"Does he have a name? Where is he from?"

Stan looked at me and shook his head. He waved his drink around the bar. He leaned into me and whispered. "He owns this place. I thought if I were here hanging out here, I'd pick up on something. Never have. His name is Henkle. Henkle Schlygel. Schlygel means hammer in German. Thus, the name of this place."

"I'll see what I can do."

A shrill voice came from the doorway. "Stan honey, we're all waiting for you. I'm starving!" Stan looked at the woman in the bar's doorway, her hands on huge hips. He waved to her.

"See what I mean? Does she look the least bit like she's starving? Thanks for your help. Let me know if I can give you anything else, Chief."

Stan left to attend to his wife and guests. I looked at my watch. It was time for Ellen to get off work. I paid my bill and looked for her. She had changed clothes and was standing by the front door. I put my hand on her shoulder.

"Don't touch me," she said as she faced away and knocked my hand off her shoulder. She continued to look out the window. "I saw you with your business associate - rubbing her leg against you, and the two of you whispering."

"It's all part of the game. That's how we keep our discussions secret. The others think we're just lovers, not in business. The work we do requires discretion."

"Some discretion. Now everyone will think I'm going out with a two-timer. No thanks." She stared at me. She didn't move her lips, but I heard her say, "*I'm tired of you being a victim. You need to help yourself. At least try to get better.*" Why did I keep hearing those voices?

"Let me take you home and we can talk about it on the way."

"I called a cab already. Just go. I don't want to look at you."

47

10

It looked like I lost my chance with Ellen, at least for now. I concentrated on my job and was flawless in my execution. Every package on time and in perfect condition, delivered to the recipient. I had been doing it for three weeks.

The cash appeared in Arry's glove box every night. How she managed to get it in there when I wasn't looking was beyond me. Yet, it was there and it was a lot.

I had to find places to stash it all. I didn't want it all in one place if my house was robbed. Some in the Captain Crunch and some in the bottom of the clothes hamper. I had to learn how to launder it and move out of my shithole of a house, excuse me, my worn-out domicile.

I knew I would solve my problem soon when I received a text for my next drop at the end of the day. The name was, Henkle Schlygel - the owner of the Velvet Hammer Stan spoke about. Now I had a place to find him. Maybe he'd talk to me when I delivered his package.

He was at the top of a high-rise office building. After I entered the elevator and tried to press the button for the top floor, I couldn't. There was a keyhole next to it and the button wouldn't push in. I stepped off the elevator and looked around. There was a guard at the lobby desk reading a paperback. I walked over to him with my fancy package.

"I need to get to the top floor and there's a key access which, of course, I don't have."

He looked at me suspiciously. He wasn't one of those doughnut security guards. He looked in shape and intelligent with some gray in his black hair. Weathered skin spoke of his rugged past along with a slash of a scar on his face. "Who are you trying to see? What for?"

"I have to deliver this package to Henkle Schlygel."

"Give it to me. What's in it?"

"I don't know."

"How do you know Henkle Schlygel is here?"

"I was told to come here."

"By whom? No one knows he's here. His name is nowhere, he doesn't own anything here. Why not try a business he owns like the Velvet Hammer or any of his several other businesses in his name? I think you have the wrong address."

"No. I have to deliver it personally. It's part of my job. It isn't the wrong address and the fact that I have it right must tell you something. Something like, you need to get me upstairs to see him."

He looked around and sighed. "Shit. I was hoping to be done for the day already. Okay. Let's get this going. Follow me."

He took me into a back room and placed the package on an x-ray table. I could see the contents on the monitor at the bottom of the box. It looked like some kind of crystal standing up on a base - like a display piece.

He mumbled. "Fancy. Okay, let's see if it's a bomb." He took some tongs, wiped the box with a white pad, and put it into a machine. A green light lit. "Okay, we'll clear you at the top floor. Come on."

He led me to the elevator and inserted his key. The top floor button lit up and he pushed it. We stared at the floor indicator lights as we went up. The doors opened to a brightly lit, secure area, with whitewashed cement walls, white tile floors, and another set of security with video cameras, an x-ray conveyor, and a metal detector followed by an x-ray walk through.

He walked over to the machines and started them all up. When he was done he waved me to go through. "Package on the belt. Remove any objects from your pockets and place them on the belt then walk through."

He stood by the machines. I heard Ekaterina in my head, *"These are only tests. They need to be thorough."* I walked through to the other side and grabbed my things. I asked, "I didn't see any monitor for the x-rays. Where are the x-ray monitors?"

"They're in Mr. Schlygel's office. He has the entire floor. He, or someone working for him, has been watching us since I put the key in the elevator." He pointed to the cameras mounted on the ceiling. "You can take your things and the package and wait by the door. It'll open soon. I'm going back down."

He turned and left. I stood before the door. It was huge. Stainless steel on huge hinges. It looked like a bank vault, or blast door on a missile silo. It hissed and opened. A tall, powerful looking man in his thirties with dark skin and hair, clean-shaven and neat in a black pinstriped suit, stood in the opening. He held his hand out. "I'll take that."

"No. I have to deliver it personally."

"You can't. Just give it to me." He reached for it.

I held it back from him and started talking quickly. "Look. It's all been checked out. He tested it and it's been x-rayed and everything. Didn't you see it on the monitors? Haven't you been watching? I get paid a thousand bucks every time I deliver one of these and that's because it's special and our customers are of the highest caliber. I can't give it to you. I have to deliver it directly. The sender, who more than likely is a very close personal friend of your boss, wouldn't allow it. I'm sure your boss would be upset if his buddy spent all that money and effort to get him a gift and then have you screw it up. If they wanted to do that, they could have used UPS.

I'm telling you. You don't want the ramifications of having this package sent back and you can't take it to him, I have to." The sweat dripped from my armpits. My heart was racing. I heard Ekaterina, *"Calm down, dear, your blood pressure and heart rate are up."* Hearing that did calm me. Where was it coming from?

He looked me up and down. "Put the package on the floor, your hands against the wall, and spread your legs."

I did as I was told. He frisked me thoroughly, ran his finger around my collar, and put his hand inside my shirt. Then he ran a beeping wand over my body. When he was done, he let out a sigh. "Okay. Pick up the package."

I did. He took a pistol out of his holster under the back of his suit-coat and pressed it against my head. He grabbed my ear tight in his other hand. "Don't do anything sudden or stupid and we'll both be fine."

We walked down the blank, blisteringly white corridor that seemed to narrow to a point. He pressed his gun against the back of my head as he held my one ear. The corridor was filled with cameras, and what appeared to be black metal tubes on swivels that followed us as we walked. I heard him behind me, "A little farther. Those are machine guns following us, if you hadn't noticed. If he doesn't like what he sees, we're both dead."

We stopped at a point in the wall that looked like the rest of it - solid. He turned me to face the wall. A piece of the wall slid back and to the side. A red carpet led to a huge desk separated from us with thick glass.

He walked me in and we both stood in front of the glass. Henkle Schlygel looked up at us from his desk, many feet away. Maybe forty-something, brown and blond hair, bright blue eyes that seemed to have a piercing effect. He spoke with a German accent and it came out of a speaker somewhere. "Who are you? Who is the package from?"

"I'm Dave and I'm here to deliver this package to you. I don't know who it's from."

"Yes. I heard that before. What friend of mine would put me through this when they know the level of my security? I hope they are a dear friend, or they may not be a friend anymore. Open the package and show it to me."

"I'm not supposed to open it."

"You're opening it there, so if it blows up somehow, it's your guts and Ramone's and not mine. Open it."

I carefully took the ribbon and paper off and dropped it on the floor. I took the top off and tilted the open box toward the glass so he could see in. He approached the glass and looked inside.

His eyes opened wide. "It's beautiful. Okay. It's pulling at me. Bring it in. I have to touch it."

He walked to the side of the office and opened a glass door for us to enter. As I did, he hurriedly grabbed the box and took out the crystal. He held it tightly in his hands as he gazed at it against the light. "It's, it's beautiful!" He stood stock-still as he stared at it for a while, and then blinked several times as if mesmerized. He cleared his throat, looked around the room as if he had just arrived, and then took appraisal of us both as we stood there.

He walked over to his desk and carefully put the object on the corner. He looked inside the box. He took out a card and read silently. He looked at me and then his bodyguard. "Ramone, you can go. I'd like to speak with this gentleman for a moment. Thank you for your impeccable handling of this delivery. This gentleman was right. I would have been upset if you hadn't delivered this to me personally."

Ramone bowed graciously. "You're welcome, sir. Thank you."

Ramone left the office, into the hallway.

Henkle Schlygel handed me the card.

I looked at the card. Thick, rich feeling, black with deep pressed gold letters - it had delivered by "Argus" and the delivery company name "Ekaterina." There wasn't a "from" on the card, yet he seemed the least bit disturbed by that.

He put his hand on my shoulder and looked into my eyes. His bright blue eyes seemed different since I arrived. No longer piercing, instead they were reassuring. More like Ekaterina's eyes.

His German accent still decorated his speech. "You are Argus. You do look like him. Somehow, I think there's something I can help you with. It's fortuitous you should deliver this package today. For you, as well as me. It seems Henkle Schlygel has a complete system for helping budding entrepreneurs like yourself. Have a seat and we can talk."

He led me to a conversation pit by a gas fireplace and poured us each a glass of ice water he placed on black leather coasters. Can I interest you in something else? I believe I have a well-stocked bar."

I took my water and sipped it. "No thanks. This is just what I needed. Henkle Schlygel? You say it as if you aren't he - you believe you have a well-stocked bar?"

"Well, of course I meant Henkle Schlygel as a business, not referring to someone other than I. I am he, and he is I, of course. And the name is the business. I said *believe*, since I haven't been in it in a while. Understood?" He looked a bit perturbed.

"Yes, sir. Of course. There was no "from" on that card. Do you know who sent it?"

"Of course I do. It was from a dear and close personal friend. I knew it the moment I touched it, we're so close. Shall we discuss the details you need to functionalize your profitable relationship with Ekaterina in such a cash business?" He stood and meandered over to a wall of mahogany cabinets and drawers. He looked at it, trying to determine where he was going and ended up opening a file cabinet drawer. He took out a large manila envelope, brought it over and seated himself.

"This should be a complete package of startup materials." He took the contents out and placed the pile on the table then looked through it. He put it down and sat back. "Okay, this packet contains everything needed to set up your business to clean your cash. It also has a new identity for you should you need it at some time. Evidently, the clients of Henkle Schlygel require such measures be taken for their safety."

I watched him as he turned his attention to the papers again and looked at several of them. "For your new identity I will put down the name Argus Macguire. Is that suitable?" He looked at me as he dug for a pen in his suit-coat.

"Yes, I suppose. I don't think I'll ever need it anyway."

"Good." He wrote it down on one of the papers. "You can read the details once the process is complete. A picture of you from today's security cameras will be used."

"Fine. What about the money?"

"Yes, you will own a carwash. That happens to be the business in this packet."

"And how do I wash the money with a carwash?"

"You simply make deposits in the business account and pay yourself from it. The taxes will be paid quarterly. Henkle Schlygel has access to the account in order to handle the details of taxes, expense reporting and, of course, Henkle Schlygel's fees. How much cash are you intending to deposit and at what frequency?"

"Four thousand a day."

He flipped to a folder with 'Net Funds' on the tab and looked at a table of numbers running his finger down it. "Well organized. That amount would net you twenty-eight hundred sixty-three dollars a day, after taxes, expenses, and our fees."

"Not bad. Can I have it deposited to a personal account?"

"It's all in here. A new account will be created, credit cards issued, and it will all be delivered to you by personal courier." He handed me a form to fill out. "All I need is your full legal name, address, social security number, and any other contact information. The rest my secretary will fill out and complete for you. You should have the package delivered no later than tomorrow night it appears. Quite the process."

"That's great. I can finally get out of my house. I have a good amount of cash already. What should I do with it?"

"When you get the packet, you can make a deposit at the bank to the business account. You can have it transferred from your business account to your personal account at the same time, if you like. Remember to leave some for the fees and taxes. About twenty-eight hundred to your personal account for every four thousand going into the business account."

I handed the form back. "This was simple. All things should be so easy."

He put the form on the top of the packet and inserted it all into the envelope. He tossed it on the table. "Yes, done. I'll get this going for you. Anything else?" He leaned back in his chair and rested his ankle on his knee. He looked at his shoe as if he hadn't seen it before, and raised his eyebrows a little, as if to say he liked them. He smiled and looked back at me. "No? Then have a good day. Tell Ekaterina I said hello when you see her. I evidently don't get out often due to security issues." He looked around his office.

We stood and I held my hand out.

He shook it. "Of course. A pleasure doing business with you, Dave, or Argus, as Ekaterina prefers. You can leave the way you came. I think Ramone will lead you out."

"Thanks."

11

My credit card for the business and another for personal use, checkbooks for both accounts with ATM cards, LLC paperwork with copies of the carwash purchase agreement, and so on, were all delivered. I signed for them, which made me clean and legit.

Deposited some cash and made a transfer to my personal account. Made a payment on the carwash, and was now able to make use of my earnings.

Stopped by my clothier and purchased some casual wear. I'd lost a significant amount of weight so later I dropped off a few suits to be taken in.

I settled on new place, in a better part of town, an apartment with a secured underground garage. Had my old house cleaned up and rented to a little old lady with a one hundred and twenty pound German Shepard. That should make the neighbor's dog's life interesting.

Now all I needed in my life was to get Ellen to go out with me again. My mom's birthday was coming up and I hoped she'd meet my family with me. I just needed to convince her there was nothing between Ekaterina and I.

I arrived at the Velvet Hammer after a tough day of crisscrossing the city with deliveries. Ellen was at the podium.

"Hi Ellen. How are you this lovely evening? You look wonderful, as usual."

She looked at me with a smirk. "Just fine. And you, sir?"

"Stop with the sir stuff already. What do I have to do to convince you there is nothing going on between Ekaterina and me? Do I look like a two-timer?"

She looked me up and down. "I don't know. You've lost a lot of weight. I figure it must be for her." She looked back at her reservation sheet.

"When was the last time you even saw us together? It's been weeks. And can't I improve myself? Do you know what it's like being fat as I was? It's hell. Your feet and knees hurt, you're always tired. Besides, I fit in my car better now, too. Can't I look good for you instead of for her? Why would I keep trying like this if I were with her? Think about—"

"Excuse me, sir. May I take care of my customers that just came in?"

I stepped aside. A group of highly perfumed, cackling women entered. The roundest of the group stepped up to the podium. "Reservations for the judge, please."

I heard, "*Help me get him to the private room.*"

Stan walked in behind them all. His face lit up when he saw me. He came over and put his hand on my shoulder. "Dave. Good to see you. You haven't been around lately and I was beginning to become concerned you ran into some trouble. How's the agent life going?"

Ellen maneuvered around Stan and I. "Excuse me, Judge Seymour. Right this way, Mrs. Seymour, ladies." She led them to their room, all of them cackling as they waddled away.

Stan and I watched them leave. He turned to me. "See why I take some quiet time in the bar? Come on and have a drink with me." He put his arm over my shoulder and led me to my corner.

William promptly put linen napkins down and set off for our drinks. We seated ourselves. Stan turned his stool toward mine and leaned into me. "So, anything on old Henkle Schlygel?"

"Not much. He owns more than this place, but he never goes to them. Wherever he is, I don't think we'll find him."

"Damn. We know he has other businesses, too. I guess I was hoping you guys might have a better lead or more information from your sources. Oh well. Thanks for trying."

"Sure. Always willing to help, Stan."

William put down our drinks. "Appetizers, gentlemen?"

Stan shook his head no. "Thanks William. Not much of an appetite. I have to eat with the women again tonight."

William looked at me. I said, "Certainly. No Foie gras, though."

"At once. Wine?"

"No thank you. This will do."

"Of course, Sir David." He ran off.

Ellen came over, almost next to us, as Stan turned back to me. "Have you learned anything else about our mystery woman? We haven't seen her here in a while."

Ellen stood politely, waiting for Stan to look at her.

I said, "Sorry, I don't know anything about her. Still a mystery."

"I think she has something evil going on. You stay out of harm's way now."

"Excuse me, Judge Seymour," Ellen quietly prompted.

"Yes, dear. What's wrong?" Stan put his hand on her shoulder and engaged her eyes.

"It seems the ladies want to eat. Your wife says she's going to faint if she doesn't get some sustenance and that I should come in here and tell you it's time to quit working and take care of her."

Stan laughed and smiled at me. "See what I mean? Sorry, old boy. I guess I have to do my duty and get the ladies fed. As if any of them couldn't survive for weeks on their generous reserves."

"Have fun."

Ellen promptly left and led Stan away. I waited for her by her podium.

"Ellen. So, what I was going to ask you was, if you'd honor me at our family's gathering to celebrate my mother's sixtieth birthday. My whole family will be there and you can evaluate whether someone from a family like mine would ever be a two-timer."

She looked at me. I thought she might be biting. She swayed her head around a little - she looked so cute. "Uh, when is it? I might be busy."

"This Saturday."

She let out a sigh. "Okay, I'll go. It would be good to meet your family. What time?"

"I'll pick you up at noon. Dinner is at one o'clock."

"Deal. Tomorrow. Noon." She resisted a full smile, though her cheeks and eyes showed it. I tried to plant a kiss on her cheek - she moved away too quickly as she busied herself with the reservation list.

"Thanks," I said.

I retreated to my corner quite happy with the way I handled the judge and Ellen. The week had come to a positive ending. William delivered my appetizers. I slugged down my manhattan and tapped it on the bar to get William's attention. He came over.

"Yes, Sir David. Why the big smile? I don't think I've seen you this cheery ever."

"It's time to celebrate. This was a good week. How about another of these, my fine man? And keep them coming."

"Yes, sir!"

I dined on appetizers, thinking about what my next steps would be. Money was starting to accumulate in my business account and I would be taking draws to the personal account. I needed to find something to invest it in, so I'd have it whenever this job came to an end. If it did. I didn't like Stan's comment on Ekaterina being evil. If he's thinking like that, it might be true. Then again, he thinks I'm CIA.

As I had my fourth drink and was eating a celebration cheesecake, I smelled a most alluring scent. I heard Ekaterina speak.

"David, my love. How have you been? You look much better, by the way."

She took my attention from my plate. She wore a low cut, sheer, cream-colored, silky V-neck blouse under a black, fitted suit-coat and wore a short black skirt that matched. Her long legs crossed and she turned her seat so her leg pressed against mine. She rested her strappy, black high-heel on the rail of my seat. Her black hair fell shining across her shoulders. She kissed me on the lips as her hand rested on my thigh. I pulled back.

"Uh, uh." I tried to maneuver away, and I only threw myself off balance. She wrapped her arm around my shoulder to steady me so we wouldn't both go toppling over.

"Argus dear. Calm down. Are you okay?" She held my chin and brushed the hair from my forehead while her leg slid up and down against mine.

"Ekaterina. No. You don't know how much of a mess—"

"Now, now. As I said, calm down. There is no mess. Henkle Schlygel has taken care of everything. It appears you're well-liked by our customers and you have excellent cash flow. What could possibly be a mess?"

I looked over to the hostess station. Ellen hurriedly packed her bag up and cast me a ghastly glance as she stomped out the door.

I pointed toward Ellen. "Her. Every time I get close, you come in here and mess it all up."

She showed me a pair of pouty lips, which only made her more enticing. I became lost in her face once more while she ministered condolences by caressing my leg and running her hand through my hair while she pecked kisses on my cheek and lips. I was lost in her again. I closed my eyes to try to break loose. Tender lips were on mine and a sweet tongue entered my mouth. I ran my tongue around it and suckled it and she did the same as we kissed in some dream world.

I came to my senses and pulled away. "Shit! What happened to business? You won't even eat dinner with me, yet you'll mess up my life with anyone else?"

She moved back a few inches, still caressing me. I pushed her hands off.

"Argus, you can't become involved with her. It'll only lead to heartbreak. I'm doing you a favor. And yes, this is business. I need to protect you."

"If this is business, then why were you still kissing me after she left already?"

"People talk, dear. Trust me. Haven't I been good to you?"

She relaxed and leaned back in her seat. Her leg relaxed from pressing against mine. She took a sip of my drink. I'll leave you to enjoy your Friday night. I can see we're where we need to be right now." She stood, straightened her clothes, and ran her hand through her hair. She was gorgeous and enticing and seemed so familiar.

"Good night." She smiled and winked, turned on her heel, and walked out the door.

12

I bought an iPad for my mom at the Apple store then picked up Ellen a little past noon. She ran off the porch of the two-family apartment house when I pulled in the driveway. She was dressed in a long, flowing, summer dress with sandals. Her long shining brown hair was tied back in a ponytail. She was so cute.

I opened her door and closed it behind her. When I was in the driver's seat, she started talking immediately.

"SO. Let's get this stuff straight. The judge said you were agenting and the mystery lady was evil. Then you proceeded to suck her face while she caressed you like a lost lover. Explain." She folded her arms across her chest and stared through the windshield.

"Explain. Of course. Well, uh, first, Ekaterina is my boss. I think she thinks I look like an old lover of hers, so she seems to be attracted to me. The real reason she did that was so you could hear about it and get angry with me. She doesn't want me to be with you for some reason. She said it would only end in heartbreak. Don't worry about her, she won't even sit down to dinner with me."

Ellen unfolded her arms and fastened her seat belt. She turned to look at me while I drove. "Why would she want to keep us apart? How does she know it would end in heartbreak?"

"I don't know. The important part is, I wouldn't be trying to date you if I was interested in her. Right? I can't help what she does."

Ellen relaxed in her seat and leaned her head against the headrest. I accelerated onto the freeway and we were pushed into the seats as the engine roared to life. "That's what five hundred horses feel like," I said.

"No wait. So, you work for her. The judge said an agent. What kind of agent?"

"Well, I'm kind of an agent. He thinks I'm with the CIA for some reason though."

I couldn't tell her I was a delivery boy making a thousand dollars a box. It would raise too many questions. Questions I couldn't answer myself.

"So, are you an agent? Why would he confuse you with the CIA?"

"Oh it's just something he and William drummed up when I didn't want to tell them I worked in a factory, so I let them continue their assumptions. I think it's quite comical."

"Oh it is, is it? So now that you don't work in a factory, what do you do?"

"I have a private business. I did some studying when I worked at the factory with headphones and CDs. You know, the materials they have on Amazon? Even did some night school. I learned a few things and started a business."

"That's very exciting." She leaned toward me over the center console. "I want to know all about it."

I still had a few minutes before I made it to the safety of my mom's house. What could I possibly tell her that was believable? Maybe I could have her answer the question instead of me. "Why don't you guess?"

"Okay." She perked up, looked out the window and up at the sky. "Hmm. Agent, training from CDs, night classes, ex-factory worker makes a leap into a new world. Hot car, new address, nice clothes, and big money fast. Mystery woman as a boss. She seems to fit in to the upper crust of society well. What occupations could she have?"

She grabbed my hand on the shift lever, stretched herself toward me, and was inches from my face. "She's a hooker. No, she's the madam and you're a hooker, or a gigolo! That's why you're losing weight! You're a gigolo for rich women!" She laughed and fell back into her seat holding her belly while she kicked her feet against the floor.

I exited the freeway and pointed. "There it is. That's Mom's."

She took it in. "It's cute. All the flowers and such a perfectly manicured lawn. It looks like a golf green."

"It is. It's called bent grass. Dad's pride and joy. He has a reel style mower he cuts it with every couple of days." I pulled into the driveway behind my brother's Volvo. "Looks like my brother's already here. Always early. A true overachiever he is. Wait until you meet him. He's the prince. I'm the loser. Don't move."

I circled the car to Ellen's side and opened her door. My brother was standing on the porch with his favorite drink half gone, an Old Fashioned. "Hey little brother. Wait." His belly jiggled as he came down the steps and pointed to the car then stood by it.

"This can't be so. Did you win the lottery? And you even have new clothes. Nice button down shirt and hey, are those suit-pants? "He felt the fabric of my side pocket.

I hit his hand away. "Nothing special. I'm sure yours are better. The car's a loaner. Mine's in the shop."

He handed me his drink and patted my almost flat belly. "Lost weight, too. You look good, baby brother." He opened the driver's door and sat in Arry. "Yeah, right. Loaner. They don't loan out two hundred thousand dollar cars for someone having a fourteen-year-old rust bucket fixed." He ran his hands over the leather and then held the steering wheel looking forward. "What is this, about four hundred horse?"

"Truth be told, it's five hundred."

He turned to look at me with his mouth open and climbed out. He shook my hand. "Nice job. So what lottery was it?" I handed him his drink. He looked at Ellen standing next to me quietly. "I'm sorry, my name is John. I'm Dave's older, smarter, wiser, handsomer, nicer, and harder working brother." He stuck his hand out.

Ellen shook it. "Hi John. I'm Ellen. And no, Dave didn't win the lottery. He's been working very hard and earned it. He's been taking night classes and has become a leader in his field." She pointed to his car in front of mine. "Is that old Volvo yours? Nice, conservative, safe car. How old is it? They do last a very long time as yours is a testament to. Good choice." She smiled at him and took my arm. "Can I meet the rest of the family?"

John opened his eyes wide and smiled at her. "Very good, uh, Ellen. I think you'll fit right into this family." John wrapped his arm around her. "Let me introduce you to everyone, you sweet thing, you."

I followed them up the freshly painted white, cement stairs. The smell of spaghetti sauce wafted out the screen door. The television was competing with John's two girls fighting over how they were going to dress a Barbie doll, while his younger boy had the doll-head off one and was swinging it by the hair.

Dad was yelling for Mom. "Sophia! Your son and I need fresh drinks. How are we supposed to celebrate your birthday when we're sober, woman?" He looked back from his recliner when the screen door creaked as we entered behind him in the living room. The plastic covering on his recliner squeaked as he shifted to see Ellen under John's arm. "John, where'd you find her? Hello, young lady." He struggled his little legs to push the footrest down and nearly fell over forward as he ejected himself from his throne. He stood, looking Ellen up and down, tilting his shiny, nearly hairless head with the comb-over, and smiled under his gray mustache.

She reached a hand out. "My name is Ellen. John found me in your driveway with your handsome, charming, and successful son, Dave."

I stood behind her and smiled. "Hi, Dad. How's it going?"

"First things first, Dave. Ellen, I'm Frank." He reached out and gave her a hug. "Welcome, to our family. I'm glad you could join us today. Wish your handsome guy told me you were coming. I'd have dressed a little better." He tugged at his tee-shirt. "Oh well. I can change in a minute."

He came around Ellen and gave me a hug. "*David. My poor son, David.* You look great. Keep the woman. She's fixed you up good." He turned and yelled. "Sophia! Add another place setting to the table, we have company. And be sure to get one of the good padded folding chairs for her from the basement."

Mom came out from the kitchen with fresh drinks. She handed them to Dad and John and slid in front of me. She squeezed my cheeks, kissed me on the lips and held me at arm's length, looking me up and down. "*My baby.* You look good. Let me get you a drink. Some whiskey? Oh, you don't drink whiskey."

"Whiskey's fine, Mom." I kissed her cheek. "Need any help?"

"No, no. You'd just get in the way. Betty is back there with me and we're bumping butts already. You watch the kids play with the rest of them. I'll be back with the drinks. Ellen, welcome to our family. We'll talk later, sweetie."

Mom ran off in her sneakers and cotton housedress to the kitchen.

Dad and John were lusting over Ellen while Dad held her ponytail in one hand and stroked it with the other. "Nice shine and color. You're not Italian, though, are you? My son has brown hair too and it should be black. His skin's too light, but he's all Italian."

Ellen raised an eyebrow. "Italian? Sorry, I'm not. I'm a mix of things."

He let her silky, brown hair go. "I guess that's okay. You're still a pretty girl. I'll bet you're a good cook, too. What kinds of breads do you bake?

"Bake bread?"

"You look like you're Catholic. You're not Jewish are you? I don't see it in you."

I had to save her. "Dad, Ellen doesn't need the third degree. Besides, who cares what nationality or religion she is, and if she can cook?"

He shook his head. "I care, that's all. Just making conversation, son. It's what polite people do when they meet someone for the first time. It's polite."

It seemed Dad said, *"Ellen, how come he's lost so much weight?"* but I never saw his lips move and Ellen didn't seem to hear it.

John had to chime in. "Check his car out, Dad. It's worth more than this house is." He pointed out the door. My dad waddled over and looked out. "Mother Mary! What is that thing? Wow!"

He turned back, looked me up and down, and then looked at Ellen. He gave her a hug and a kiss. I didn't see his lips move, but I heard him say, *"You're taking good care of my son. Thank you. Someone needed to."*

Ellen smiled at my grinning dad. "I didn't buy it for him."

Mom came back with drinks for Ellen and I. "Old fashioned for Davey and a nice glass of Chianti for the pretty girl." She handed them off and ran back to the kitchen before we could say thanks.

My dad sipped his drink then responded to Ellen. "I don't care. He never had money, never did anything right, never had good grades, was gonna make his money in pro sports, with no real plan B, and now look at him. You met him and he's a changed man. Thank you."

Ellen said, "No, it's true. He did it all himself. He's an agent now and a big success."

John needed to sound smart now. It wasn't good for his little brother to show him up after all these years. "An agent, huh? Okay now it makes sense. You took some two-bit class on real estate and got lucky. Must have had some good contacts somewhere. That's the only way real estate agents get into the big commission deals."

"Right, John. Real estate." Ellen said.

He looked at me. "Looks like God takes care of the meek, just like in the Bible. I guess my brother must have been a better man after all. Lucky guy. Who else could be such a dismal failure and end up like this? Something's not right, though, with this quick success. Even if you handled real estate for the rich."

The noise level of the kids on the floor had risen to a new height. The boy had torn off all the Barbie heads and he swung them by the hair as he ran around the cramped living room in a little circle while the girls cried and waved their decapitated Barbies.

My dad shuffled himself into in the middle and grabbed my nephew by the ear. "Sammy. You know why we named you Sammy? It's so you would be a success like your great uncle the bootlegger from New York. You think he'd be doing this?" He pulled so hard on his ear he had the kid standing on his toes.

"No, Grandpa, no! He wouldn't! I heard all your stories about him. Please don't tell me them again. I'll be good." Sammy tossed the heads to the girls and they bounced and rolled on the floor as they hurried to pick them up. The room became nice and quiet, except for the television with the game on.

My dad let go of Sammy's ear, smacked the back of Sammy's head with his palm, grabbed the remote from the end-table, shut off the TV, and flipped the remote on his plastic covered throne. He lifted his glass to us. "To family." He clinked all of our glasses. "Sophia, when is dinner going to be ready? Ellen here is starving to death. She's so skinny. We need to get some meat on her bones."

Ellen forced a smile and sipped her wine. She looked up at me and pulled me down to whisper in my ear. "This should be fun. Real estate, huh? I want to go see some of the properties you're selling. I'll take the day off Monday."

"Uh."

Betty emerged from the kitchen, taking her apron off. "Dinner's ready. Everyone take your seat. I put name tags on the plates where you should sit."

Betty's carbohydrate nourished cheeks, her five-foot-two body that used to be one hundred and five pounds and was now two hundred, and her sneakers to ease the pain on her feet, spoke of her full indoctrination into the family. My mom said when you had babies you couldn't help getting fat and she was supposed to look like that.

Betty pulled my neck down to her for a hug and a kiss. "David, you look so nice. You have to tell me everything. I only caught a little of it."

She turned to Ellen, wiped her hand on her shift, and stuck it out. "I'm Betty, John's wife." Ellen took her hand and Betty gave her a hug and a kiss on the cheek.

"Nice to meet you, Betty."

"Now come and eat. You need some food." Betty waddled into the dining room, leading the way. She let her blond hair down from a tie in the back as she did, and started pointing to the seats at the table. "Kids, you're at the card table roped to ours so it doesn't fall over like last time. Sammy, don't play with the levers underneath. Ellen and David, you're on the other side, Grandpa is at the head as is proper, and Grandma in her seat by the kitchen next to Grandpa, then me, and then Johnny."

We all squeezed into our seats trying not to bang the hutch or the walls. John picked up a bowl of steaming angel-hair pasta from the table and started loading his plate. Betty put two, much smaller bowls, of meatballs and sausages into motion after she put one of each on my dad's plate. A huge loaf of sliced garlic bread steamed from the foil wrapping in the basket that Sammy brought over to their attached table. I put a bowl of black olives in motion. Ellen started filling her bowl with salad.

Dad sat down and surveyed everyone. "Anyone need a drink before we start? Sophia can get you one." Everyone was too engaged in passing the food to answer. "Ellen? More wine? Sophia. Bring the bottle of wine out here for Ellen. We need to loosen her up so she tells us her secrets."

Mom reached over Ellen's shoulder and poured some of Dad's homemade Chianti for her, filling her glass. She put the label-less, chipped bottle down in front of her. "It's right there for you now dear." She patted Ellen's shoulder.

I put three sausages, a meatball, and a small dollop of pasta on my plate. I immediately caught hell for it from my mom. "David! That's not how we eat. Such a little pile of pasta. That's a child's size. And why all the meat? It's bad for you."

"Oh ma. I'm trying to get down to a normal weight."

"You need to put on some more. You've gotten too thin. What's happened to you? Look at your brother," she said with a piece of garlic bread in one hand pointing it to him. "You should be more like him. You should have been an engineer and married a nice Polish girl like Betty. Look how nice they look together. Betty looks like a real mom, now that she's put on some weight, and John is looking more and more like your father."

John smiled a, 'see, I'm better than you' smile at me and winked while his cheeks puffed with pasta as he chewed.

I couldn't get into one of these arguments with them. I thought they'd be happy seeing Ellen and the changes in me. Johnny was still the prince. Firstborn male in an Italian family is always the prince. "You're right, Mom. I'll pick up some cannoli for Ellen and me on the way home."

"Oh David. You know you can take some of mine. I'll make you a box later. So, the real estate business is good. Why aren't you in the factory anymore? It was good steady work with plenty of overtime."

"Ma, I studied and found this job. It pays more and is clean and more interesting. Isn't that a good thing?"

My dad hopped in after he swallowed his bread. "Sophia, leave the boy alone. He has a car worth more than our house and a pretty girl."

My brother shook his head, wiped sauce off his chin with the back of his hand. "Yeah, engineers can't even make money like that. What are you pulling down in this..." He cleared his throat and continued, "real estate job?"

"Enough," I said as I cut up my last sausage.

John persisted while looking at the ceiling with a fork full of dripping pasta he pointed up where he was looking. "So, what properties have you sold? What do you get? Seven percent commission? Let's see, if that car cost two hundred thousand, then you had to sell about two million eight in property to buy it with your commissions, not considering taxes."

Mom chimed in, "Isn't my Johnny smart? How quick with his numbers. He's always been so smart."

John smiled at her. "Thanks, Mom." He turned his attention back to me. "Or, you could be making payments on it. Payments and insurance would be about..." He looked at the ceiling. "Hmm, about four thousand a month, for five years. That's more than you made in your old job each month. You're not still living in your old house are you? They'd steal that car."

I rolled my eyes. Why did I go there? My brother wasn't going to let up until he found out what I was doing. "No, I moved to Winslow Towers."

"Winslow Towers? Shit! That's three grand a month right there. C'mon little brother. You're dealing dope aren't you? If you are, I'll find out, so tell me now."

Dad came to the rescue. "Johnny, Sophia, let's eat. Enough questions. Who cares what David is doing? Not all of our family was on the right side of the law and they all did well. Enough questions."

Johnny had my dad's response. "Just making conversation. Can't I ask a few questions?"

My mom tried to change the focus. "So, Ellen. Tell us how you two met. And please, take some pasta."

Ellen had finished her salad and was sipping her wine. She put it down. Mom stood and shoveled a ball of pasta on her plate. "Oh no, oh, thank you. That's good. Uh, we met at the Velvet Hammer. David is a regular there."

My brother leaned toward me shaking his forked pasta at me. "The Velvet Hammer? That's where all the rich people go. The guy that owns it is a recluse no one ever sees. You're up to something illegal David."

"I'm not, honest, I'm not. That's where I made the connections though, for my business. You wouldn't understand it, so I'm not explaining it to you."

Ellen rolled some pasta on a fork and pointed it at John, demonstrating her ability to adapt to the family's method of talking. "David is a good friend with Judge Stan Seymour. Do you think the judge would be David's friend if he were doing something illegal? The Hammer has a lot of prominent people going to it."

Dad dropped his utensils on his empty plate with a clatter and grabbed his belly. "Full! Nice meal, Sophia. Friends with a judge? Good job David. Always good to have friends on that side of the law. He was the top criminal prosecutor before he became a judge, you know. Put away a lot of your second and third cousins back then. Stay friends."

"I plan to, Dad. He's a great guy. His wife is his biggest problem right now." I laughed thinking about it.

Dad was rubbing his belly and wiping sauce from his hands onto it. "That's because he doesn't know how to handle his women. If you know how to handle them, they'll wash your feet like Sophia does. Right, dear?"

Sophia smirked and slapped his bicep. "Of course dear."

Betty piped up, "Sophia! Don't hit Poppa."

Mom countered, "Do you wash Johnny's feet?"

"Sometimes. You know..." She leaned forward and feigned whispering with her hand beside her mouth, and purposely spoke loudly, "...when they get that smell." Betty laughed.

"Oh. Okay then," Mom said.

Ellen tried to turn the conversation. "So, Frank, how do you get your lawn so perfect?"

Dad put his hand on her forearm. "Oh you noticed. Thanks for asking."

John stuck his two cents in. "He uses illegal fertilizers and pesticides he buys on the black market, like my brother's involved in. If I were you, little girl, I'd want to see the properties my brother sells."

Dinner was a trip from hell. We finished as soon as we could and left. Luckily, Ellen was tired from all the wine and pasta and needed to rest. I dropped her off at her house. We stood at the door.

"That was a nice time. I'm sorry I'm so sleepy. I think I had too much wine and pasta."

"It'll do that to ya. I'm sure the rest of my family is napping in the living room by now."

Her light green eyes were drooping as she put her wrists on my shoulder and pulled me to her. She kissed my lips. I could taste the Chianti with a trace of cannoli and coffee. Success. I had been kissed by Ellen. She leaned back. "So I'll take the day off and go with you around your properties tomorrow, right?"

"Uh, no. You better not."

"Why? If you have clients, you can say I'm your secretary. Please? It would be so neat to see these places and meet your clients."

"I can't tomorrow. The schedule is too tight. Maybe another time."

Ellen raised one eyebrow. "You aren't a drug dealer like your brother says, are you? Those numbers he was throwing around tell me how much money you make and you could be a drug dealer. I won't date a drug dealer."

"I know. I promise. I'll prove it to you, just not tomorrow okay? Now go get some rest."

"Okay, my sweet David. Call me." She released me and gave me a peck on the cheek before going in.

How could I show her I wasn't a drug dealer? I had to think of something.

13

I made deliveries Monday, all the while thinking about what to tell Ellen. Then I realized all I needed to do was show her the carwash I owned. There was a business with an address on the papers that Henkle Schlygel provided.

At a lunch of Ahi tuna and seaweed, (boy did I miss my dollar meals) I scratched out the carwash numbers to see if it could generate the cash I made. $4000 per day at $10 per wash was 400 cars a day. Two minutes per car is 800 minutes a day. 800 divided by 60 minutes per hour was 13.3 hours per day of continuous running of the wash. Not likely, but I didn't work weekends either and the carwash could, so if it was a busy wash, it might be able to do it. So it made sense being a laundry for my cash, as long as it didn't make all of that cash by itself.

I wanted to see what I bought anyway, so I could kill two birds with one stone by taking Ellen. She agreed to ride with me to see my business. I drove home, changed into my jeans and a tee-shirt, and picked her up at the Hammer.

Ralph, the valet, opened my door. "Good evening, sir."

"Good evening, Ralph. Just be a moment. I'm picking up Ellen to go for a ride."

"Yes, sir. I'll put it to the side here. Go on in."

Ellen was ready and obviously excited because she caught her bag up on the podium and nearly toppled it. "Oh gosh. Thanks for catching it. Let's see what you have to show me."

She waited for me to open her door. Her jeans clung to her lithe body and the tininess of her waist was a testament to her eating habits. I continued to lose weight and would soon be at my ideal weight and be able to have all my clothes either altered or replaced permanently. I heard my mother say, *"Oh David, my baby, you're getting too thin, Mother Mary, help us."*

A hand grasped my shoulder. It was Stan. He whispered in my ear. "I see you're in a hurry. I won't be a second. Henkle Schlygel contacted me and he said, after a conversation with you, and a life of living in hiding, he wants to make a deal. He's going to provide a list of all the drug dealers' real addresses, accounts, and everything he has on them so we can monitor them and lock them up. I'm meeting with the DA tonight and he's taking it to the Chief of Police. Thanks for your help. Does the CIA want a part?"

"Uh, sure. No problem Stan. No, let the local group take the credit."

"Thanks Dave. We'll talk later. Go ahead and enjoy the night with Ellen. Hello, Ellen. Sorry for the interruption."

"No problem, Judge."

I opened the door and she ran out to the car.

Shit. Now what? Why would this guy give all his customer names out after I talked to him? We never talked about that. I wondered if I was on that list. He knew Ekaterina, so why would she let that happen? Crap. I could hear Ekaterina as if she were there, *"David dear, you'll be okay. You have to be."*

Ralph opened Ellen's door. I walked around Arry and slid in my side. "Have a good evening," Ralph said, and then shut her door.

Ellen put her bag behind the seat and buckled up.

"I like Judge Seymour. He's such a nice, orderly old man."

"Yes, he is. See. Like you said at my mom's, how could I be involved in illegal deals if he's such a good friend?"

"I guess. Sometimes I'm right and sometimes I'm wrong. So, we're going to see your carwash. I'm so excited. Where did you say it was?"

"Just about an hour outside of town. It's on the GPS."

Ellen touched the GPS screen and it lit up as I pulled away. It started calling out directions in the pleasant British woman's voice I chose to use.

"I don't see the address."

"Touch the menu button and then current route."

She started touching buttons and all the addresses I had programmed in since I started deliveries, were scrolling by. "Oops. Why do you have so many addresses? Are these real estate deals you're working on?"

"Uh, yeah some of them."

"Turn left in one hundred meters," called my familiar voice.

"This one's for the federal building. It's not for sale. Is that where you picked up a client?"

"Yes, of course, must have been. Let me get the address for you while we're at the light."

I took over the GPS, showed her the address, and put it back on the map.

"It's quite a way to Unionville. Can't be many customers for a carwash there."

"Enough to make money."

We drove with Ellen playing with the satellite radio and talking about her day and her plans for the future, in a vision I could see us in, until we reached the carwash. We pulled in.

"That can't be it!" she said.

It was a two stall, wand type carwash with the hoses broken off the wall and a stray sheep from the farm next door sitting on the ground in one of them. The rusty signs hung crooked from the half hanging overhead doors.

"Uh, must have gotten the wrong address."

"Come now. Is this the address on the papers?"

I took the title out of the glove box where I put it after I put it in the GPS. I handed it to her. She read it.

"Either you've been ripped off or something else is going on."

"Uh, ripped off."

"So how do you make all the money you spend? I tried to look up your real estate license and you don't have one in this state. How can you do business here? I even checked surrounding states."

"You investigated me? Ellen, I'm shocked."

"David. Where did you get this title?"

"Uh." I shrugged my shoulders. The sweat was dripping from under my arms. Now what?

"Take me home. I'm tired of your evasion and lies. You're not telling me because you're doing something illegal. I don't want to talk about it anymore and stop calling me. And please don't come into the Velvet Hammer anymore."

"But Ellen."

She crossed her arms and looked out the side window. "Home, driver. I'm tired."

14

I was at a loss as to what to do about Ellen. She was fed up with not knowing what was going on with me. I wanted to ease her mind, but I was helpless.

I did my deliveries every day and avoided going to the Velvet Hammer. After about three weeks of this, and not seeing Ellen or being able to get her out of my mind, I braved the Velvet Hammer one Saturday night.

Ellen was at her podium. When she saw me enter, she looked at her reservation sheet.

"Hi," I said.

No reply. Her head twitched some as she pointed at the reservations with her pencil like a doctor with her patient's chart.

I walked closer and stood at the podium. "Ellen. It's me. Will you accept an apology?"

She looked up at me with her lips flattened against each other and fire in her eyes. "Apology? For what? Being a compulsive liar? So what if you did? Would it ever change you? I think not, David. Excuse me, you may enter the bar if you like." She leaned around me to see the customers behind me. "May I help you?"

I walked into the bar. William greeted me with a wide smile. "Sir David! So good to see you. It has been some time since I last had the pleasure of your company. Would you like the usual?"

"Absolutely William."

"Appetizers sir?"

"Not yet. I don't seem to have much of an appetite."

"Of course. Maybe after a drink or two."

William busied himself with my drink. I stared at him as he prepared it and my mind was a complete blank. I was at a loss as to what to do. Here I was banking tons of money, having everything falling into place in my life, except the one person I needed to satisfy. Ellen.

William set my drink on a folded linen napkin before me. "Something the matter, Sir David? You appear to be somewhat disturbed, if you don't mind my saying."

I lifted the drink to William and took a sip. "No, I don't mind. I'm at a loss as to what to do about Ellen."

"Ah, a problem with the ladies. Those do tend to make one feel the worst. Maybe if you talk it out, an answer will come. I'm all ears if you'd like some counseling. Of course, completely confidential. Is it a problem with your sexual relations with her? Many men in here have some dysfunction due to their age. You seem too young for that."

I laughed. "No, no dysfunction here. At least I don't think so. It has been some time." I thought about the last time. It was in high school for God's sake. What a stud.

"That's good to hear. Maybe something more of a mismatch in life views?"

"Not that. More of a trust issue, I think."

"Ah, she saw you with the mystery woman."

"Yes, but that's not it. We'd gotten past that and she knows Ekaterina was just trying to keep us apart. It's more related to what I do for a living. I can't tell her the truth and I'm not so sure what I can do about it."

"Ah, I see. Yes, that is a problem. Doesn't the agency have some way to create covers for their agents?"

"Covers for undercover work, but not for creating an all-encompassing life."

"I see." William polished a glass as he looked up at the ceiling. "These things have a way of working themselves out sir. Just relax and see. Enjoy your drink and imagine it working out."

Stan showed up to my right and took the seat next to me. "David. So good to see you. I've been wondering how you've been doing." I looked at him and even though his lips didn't move I heard him say, "*Roll him over.*"

My heart started racing. Stan had the list of all of Henkle Schlygel's clients last time I saw him. I was hoping I wasn't on that list. Would he be here to take me away and lock me up?

"I've been busy." My armpits started to sweat. "How've you been?"

Stan waved at William and they exchanged sign language for him to get Stan a drink. Stan looked at me and took a deep breath. He shook his head. "I don't know how to best tell you this."

Oh, shit. Here it comes.

Ellen came into the bar to get a group for their dinner reservation and stood by us as she caught their attention in the other corner where they were all rising to follow her. She was close enough to hear Stan.

"Your work with Henkle Schlygel has already netted us two of the major drug dealers. It won't be long before everyone on the list is captured. Knowing their actual locations and names was a big help. All we had to do was track them for a while and they were caught. They'll be off the streets soon. Thanks to you and your organization's help."

Ellen looked at us with her eyes wide open after overhearing what Stan said. Maybe that would help her to accept me. The bigger problem was if I was on that list.

"I'm glad I was able to be of some help. It's a great thing you've done with that information. Congratulations Stan. Are all the names on the list drug dealers?"

"Henkle Schlygel only gave me the names of drug dealers and illegal gun traffickers - ones posing a danger to him personally. I can understand he wouldn't want to completely wipe out his customer base and we did give him immunity should any of his other customers get caught and turn him in. We don't care about the rest of them. At least they're paying taxes and their businesses aren't killing people."

It felt like a rush of cool air flooded over me. I wiped the sweat from my brow with my drink napkin. "That's great to hear, Stan."

"Well, son, it wouldn't have been possible without your help. Thanks for talking him into assisting us. I think you helped him realize how much better his life could be if these guys were off the street and not a potential threat to him should something go wrong. Soon he'll be able to live freely without all of his security."

"It did take some talking. You're welcome."

"Well, take care. I need to get going," Stan said, and then shook my hand and left.

Ellen returned to stand before me with her happy, light green eyes wide open. She stood on her toes and whispered in my ear. "I'm so sorry. I didn't realize it could be true that you were some sort of secret operative." She kissed my cheek. "Want to go out this weekend?"

15

I continued deliveries that week. One delivery completely caught my attention that something strange was going on. It was a delivery to a very nervous and twitchy person.

He was the head of the transit system for the city. A sprawling system of decaying equipment with potential for terrorist threats, and a nightmare of security concerns.

I arrived at his office on my third delivery that day after an almost carb-free lunch of a steak with veggies and an iced tea. His corner office was on the third floor in an old city government building. I arrived after a ride on an old elevator with sliding, gold-painted gates, and an elevator operator on his stool.

The worn oak door had a frosted window with his name painted on it in black letters. I turned the brass knob and was standing in front of a secretary's desk that looked like it came out of a Bogart movie.

A smiling, twenty-something woman was filing her fingernails as she looked up at me. "Oh hi! Here to see Jack?"

"Yes, good afternoon. As a matter of fact, I am."

"Good. He could use a break. He doesn't get many visitors unless someone comes to complain. You're not complaining are you?" She put the file down, stood, and brushed her blond hair back over her shoulders.

"Nope. I have a gift to deliver to him."

"Good. Maybe that'll cheer him up. He's such a nice guy. Follow me." She turned and led the way in her jeans and cotton blouse. She knocked twice on the open door and said, "Jack, you have a visitor."

"Great, Jennifer. I guess I need to get it over with. Come in."

He sat behind his desk. His left hand raced from his forehead across the back of his scalp, over and over while he looked at me with fear in his eyes, his right eye was twitching continuously. His right hand jerked nervously, rolling a pencil back and forth between thumb and forefinger. He tried to lay it on his desk and it spun and landed on the floor behind it.

He stood, kicking his chair back on its rollers as he did, and knocked his head as he dove under the desk to retrieve it. He rose and placed the pen on the desk, then reached his hand out. "I'm Jack, the name that was on the door. How can I help you?"

I shook his sweaty palm as he gave me a twitching, limp fish of a hand and his eyes blinked rapidly at me as he waited in fear.

"Good afternoon Jack. I have a gift to deliver to you." I held the gold-wrapped package out to him.

He pulled back and held his shaking hands out, palms facing it. "No no. Take it away. Someone's probably trying to kill me. It's probably a bomb."

"No sir. I can assure you it isn't a bomb. It's a gift. A lovely gift. You can open it while I'm here, if that's any reassurance." I held it before him as he looked at it.

"Okay that makes sense. You wouldn't want to blow up with it, would you? What is it?"

"I'm not sure. I deliver packages from special clients. Everyone who gets them is happy with them though."

"A special client? Who would want to give me a gift? Everyone hates me."

"I'm not sure, sir. Family? Friends?"

"I don't have any." He looked at me and then Jennifer. "Except Jennifer. She's been a gift."

She smiled at him. "Gee, thanks Jack. You never said that before."

Jack looked at her. "Is it from you?"

"I should have surprised you now that I think of it. Sorry, though. Open it and let's see what it is and who it's from." Jennifer took it from my hands and placed it on the desk in front of Jack.

Jack looked at the package as it sat there. He tentatively placed his left hand on it and pulled the loose end of the bow. The ribbon fell free. He tore at the gold paper and the box was free. He lifted the lid, turned his head to the side to look at it with only one eye, as if it might squirt him, and peered inside. "It's nice. So, uh, I have to take it out. I can't resist the feeling."

His hand shook as he reached into the box and grasped the crystal and its base. He lifted it and looked at it with the sunlight behind it from the floor-to-ceiling window. His eyes locked on it and he became motionless. No twitching. His hands were still. His breathing slowed. After a few moments, he cleared a spot for it on his desk and placed it carefully and reverently on the corner.

Jennifer reached into the box, removed the card, and read it out loud. "Ekaterina. Delivered by Argus." She looked at me. "Are you Argus?"

"Yes, I am. I work for Ekaterina's delivery service."

She looked at the card again. Jack was calm and patient while he watched her. "There is no 'from'." Jennifer looked at me then to Jack.

Jack smiled. "Don't worry. I know who it's from. It's a close personal friend. Someone who hasn't been around for a long while." He took the card and dropped it back into the box. He put the wrapping and ribbon in it and tossed it into his trashcan alongside the desk. He started to organize his desk then remembered we were still there. He stopped and said, "Argus, Thank you for your services today. I'll be sure to tell Ekaterina how well you've done." He paused and blinked several times as if he was distracted. He looked around the office. "Transit system. Tell me Argus, have you dealt with the transit system in this city?"

"Yes, I have."

"What do you think about it? Your honest opinion."

"I think it should be in better shape given all the revenue it generates."

Jennifer looked at him as if he were wearing a costume. "Jack, you've heard all the complaints before. Why are you asking?"

"Of course I have." He paused again staring out the window perfectly still. He turned back to Jennifer. "And I know why it's that way. It's all the fingers in the till of the system. The corruption is killing it. I can handle it now, though."

Jennifer's eyes widened. "Jack, are you okay? I've never seen you this way."

He put his hand gently on her shoulder. He looked calmly into her eyes. "This gift has given me new purpose. It reminds me of what I used to be. I should take you to dinner tonight. Would you honor me by accepting my invitation?"

"Jack, my, uh, I."

"We can discuss the plans I have to correct the transit system. I think you deserve a raise, as well. You'll be much busier once the department has money to spend."

He turned to me. "Argus." He reached his hand out. "Thank you again. I'm sure you have other gifts to deliver and I don't want to keep you."

He had a firm grip and his palm was dry. "Yes, of course. Thank you."

I left the building and headed to the parking garage. The acrid and foul smells of the city filled my senses as I walked lost in thought. The smell of urine from the homeless, the diesel fumes from the buses.

I had to find out what was happening with these gifts. All the recipients seemed transformed by them. None could resist touching it once they saw it. Once they did, they changed.

I thought about Henkle Schlygel - how he decided to clean up all the drug dealers and gun traffickers. How Jack had lost all of his maladies and was now fearless as he set about eliminating corruption in the transit system.

Other deliveries had similar results. They all weren't as obvious as Jack's, with his severe fear and nervousness. Were they all transformed somehow into better, more courageous and altruistic people? It seemed to be. What could have possibly caused it? If these were gifts the people recognized as being from a close personal friend, they must all have some very special close personal friends.

I drove Arry to the next pick-up and drop-off and saw similar results in the recipient's transformation. The more deliveries I made, the more they told me their plans, and all their plans included cleaning up harmful elements of society. I needed a drink to think about everything. My last stop done, I drove to the Hammer. How I wished I could speak to Ekaterina.

16

Ellen was in a light blue flowered dress with heels and a matching flower on the side of her head. Her eyeshadow matched the light green of her eyes and she smelled like heaven as I leaned in for a kiss.

"David. You surprised me."

"Ellen."

"This weekend we're trying something new. Right?"

"Absolutely. That reminds me. I haven't told Ekaterina yet."

"Don't forget."

"I won't."

"Dinner later?"

"Sorry, I have a lot going on that I have to think about. Afraid I wouldn't be good company."

Ellen pouted then touched my hair, moving it to the side on my forehead. "That's okay." Her eyes flitted around my face taking me in like a drug. "I understand your job now. I trust you. I love you."

"I love you, too."

"Okay, go ahead and do what you do."

I walked into the bar and William promptly brought me my usual. "Good evening, Sir David. Pleasant day?"

"Yes. Just have a few things to think about and it will be wrapped like a gift."

"That's a nice way to phrase it. I'll let you think then. If you should desire anything, let me know."

"Thank you."

It felt good to have a place to go to like the Hammer. It was like coming home; being greeted by Ellen, then to be doted over by William taking impeccable care of me. It was all good.

Now, it may be even better. Before, I wasn't so sure about the morality of what I was doing. It seemed impossible to do something for so much money, without it being illegal. Now, it seemed it wasn't illegal and it was beneficial to society. I was helping to right the wrongs in the world by the gifts I delivered and the effects on the people receiving them. How did it work?

I finished my first drink rather quickly and as I looked for William, Stan walked in and came over. A broad smile covered his wrinkled face and his silver eyes gleamed as he approached me. He clapped me on the back then grabbed my hand and shook it with both of his. He leaned in and spoke quietly, "The world is becoming a much better place because of you. We have all the people on the list. My court schedule is filled with drug dealers and gun peddlers. Many lives will be saved. You're my personal hero."

"Oh Stan, stop. Thanks. It's not a big deal."

"This is a big deal. I just wish I could blow your cover and let the world know."

"That wouldn't be good."

"I understand."

William approached, took my glass, and commenced to make another.

I turned to Stan as he seated himself next to me. "Have you ever heard of people having dramatic life changes? Things that change their very being and makes them a better person and eliminates all of their maladies and fears?"

Stan sipped his drink and put it down still holding it. "Sounds like a miracle. Would make both of our jobs a lot easier wouldn't it?"

"Yes. Think about it though, what might do such a thing?"

"Why, have you seen it?"

"Henkle Schlygel, for one."

"That was from your talk with him, I'm sure."

"Maybe. Sometimes people improve themselves."

"Of course. You know, I saw a show the other night on one of those educational channels. Being around my wife, I need to have some intelligent stimulation like we're having now. Anyway, it was about paired particles that can be separated many miles and yet, when one is stopped, or reversed in rotation, the other follows. Like a remote control. Then, I saw a show on psychology and how they eliminated maladies from people by altering their DNA. Then there was another show that spoke about the influence of color on one's thoughts and behavior." He sipped his drink.

"I'm not sure where you're going with this."

"Me either. I guess the point I was making was there is so much we don't know. I guess anything is possible. As long as it's positive, why question it?"

"No questions?"

"If it works out for the good, who cares?"

"Wouldn't you want to know?"

"Not necessarily. Why tie your mind up unless, of course, it's for entertainment value." Stan put his empty on the bar and stood. "I have to go now. The wife is at her friend's, the house is quiet and there's a good show on I want to watch in peace. Good seeing you David." He shook my hand and patted my shoulder.

"Thanks Stan. And thanks for the advice."

"No problem."

Stan left. William came over. "Appetizers Sir? Wine?"

"No to the wine. Another Blanton's and the appetizers, minus the foie gras."

"Right away, Sir David."

I finished my drink, still befuddled by what happened. I was never very good at taking advice. I never took my mom's and my dad's and I ended up in a factory. Now I had what I wanted and I was still questioning good advice from a smart man telling me to not worry about it. I was being stupid, but I knew somehow, something had to be wrong with my deliveries regardless how good the results were.

William brought the appetizers and my drink. I dug in, wrapped in my thoughts.

As I finished my third Manhattan, which had a greater effect on me since I had lost weight, I was relaxed, a little buzzed, and felt as if my mind would be able to answer the question shortly. I smelled something alluring.

"Hello, Argus."

She was seated already and had slid her silky leg against mine. Her hair was pulled back tight, giving her facial features even more drama. I took in her high cheekbones and dramatic eyes. Her painted lips were a luscious wet red. She wore a short sequined cocktail dress that revealed her long legs in her sky-high heels. Her face was almost touching mine.

My eyes closed voluntarily. A kiss graced my lips and melted me inside. I came to my senses and pulled away. Why was I so in love with this woman?

"Ekaterina. You look stunning tonight. Please don't call me Argus."

"Okay, David. Yes, I know. Cocktail party with friends. Old friends."

"Would you like a drink? By the way, I'd like to take off Monday and Tuesday if that's okay and I have questions for you."

"No thanks on the drink. Vacation is fine. I just came in to work on your Ellen situation. I need to have you two break it off." She ran her hand up and down my thigh. I stopped her and she wrapped her long fingers in mine.

"Tell me, what's in the packages? Why do people lose their maladies, fears and become champions for bettering the world?"

She ran her hand through my hair and rested it on my shoulder as she leaned into me. "What does it matter? They received a gift."

"Yes, but is there some kind of drug or power in the crystal? Is it just because a close personal friend gives them a wakeup call with the gift? What makes it work?"

"Take my advice. It will do you no good to question this. Moreover, don't ever think about touching the crystal yourself. It could cause nearly irreparable damage. You need to start taking advice and conforming."

"Conforming."

"Yes, you never listened to your mom telling you to study and get good grades, you never listened to your dad telling you to not be so lazy. Then, you came in here, conformed to their dress code, and took elocution lessons on my advice. You seemed to be heading in the right direction. Hasn't life been better for you since you did?"

I stared at her. How did she know my past? Ekaterina looked lovingly at me as if I were someone she cared deeply for. It was as if we'd always been together. She leaned into me, and kissed me quickly. She looked at her watch. "Come with me. I only have a few minutes before I have to leave."

She stood and held my hand. We walked to where Ellen stood at her podium. I could feel her eyes on me as Ekaterina wrapped her arms around me and kissed me again.

Ellen pulled Ekaterina from me. "Leave! You are not welcome here anymore. If you come in, I'll call the police," Ellen said as fire burned in her light green eyes.

Ekaterina composed herself. "How dare you touch me, you nuisance. Stay away from my husband."

"Husband? I've had enough of this! Why you're trying to keep us apart is beyond me. He's your employee and nothing else. Stay away from him. I love him. You can't make me jealous anymore." She turned to me and added, "David, you can put in a sexual harassment suit if you like. I'll be your witness."

Shit. My heart was racing. She called me her husband. Ellen was standing up for me.

Ekaterina looked in the mirror and fixed her lipstick while we stood there. She turned. "See you soon, David. Watch out, Ellen." She left us.

Ellen put her arms around my neck. "I know what she was doing. Just another attempt to make me jealous. I know she's not your wife, it's okay."

17

We were leaving for our long weekend after work on Friday. After my deliveries, I packed my things in Arry, changed clothes and drove to the Hammer to get Ellen. Ralph, the valet, greeted me.

"Good afternoon, Sir David. I see you've dressed down today."

"Yes. Just picking up Ellen to go on a long weekend."

"How nice. She just received your package. I assume it was your package, that is. The driver even had a car like yours."

"Package?"

I ran into the Hammer. Ellen had a gold wrapped box, identical to the ones I delivered every day, and the ribbons and paper were off and she was gazing inside. "No! Ellen, no!"

Her hand was reaching inside of it as I shoved my hand in the box and took the crystal out. She gave me a shocked look. "David, why are you doing that? I thought it was from you."

My body was immobilized. My head raced with unfamiliar memories and thoughts. I tried to compose myself while I heard a voice in my head telling me to comply. A woman's voice said, "Conform and it will be over soon, unless you resist. Relax." My heart was racing.

I stared at it as I held it to the light from the window. It was beautiful. I knew I had to resist. It felt as if there was someone else in my head. Not just a voice - an actual presence. The crystal had lost its beauty and luster and felt empty now. I placed it on the podium.

Ellen picked it up. "It's very pretty. What is it? Why did you grab it?"

I stared at her. Whatever was inside of me was in shock and very upset, yelling in my head, "No, no! I was supposed to be in her, not you. I'm not a man!"

I forcefully pushed the invader aside, returning to my normal self while I saw Ellen still looking at the object. "Are you okay, Ellen?" She put the crystal in her bag.

"I'm fine. How about you? Thanks for the beautiful gift."

"I'm fine. You're welcome." I couldn't tell her what just happened, because I wasn't sure myself and, even if I was, how could I tell her my body has been invaded by some other consciousness? I took a deep breath. The other consciousness was struggling for front stage. My heart pounded wildly in my chest and I began to get dizzy. I fought back.

It spoke to me in my head as I stared blankly at Ellen. "It can't go like this. You'll die and I'll die. You need to calm down. Your heart rate is too high."

"Get out of my head!" I shouted in my mind.

"I can't. You need to acquiesce," she said.

"I won't acquiesce. It's my body."

"Calm down before we both die. I'll leave you alone for now."

Her grip on me lessened. So, this is what I've been delivering.

There was a tug on my shirtsleeve. "Are you okay? You're sweating." Ellen wiped my brow with her pink kimono sleeve.

"Uh, yes, just thinking of what I might have forgotten before we get on the road. I'm sorry. Lost in thought."

"It's okay. Let me get my suitcase from the closet and we can go."

"I need to stop at the men's room first."

I walked into the bathroom and splashed water on my face, then held onto the sides of the sink willing myself to calm down. I took some deep breaths and felt my heart stop pounding. I dried my face and decided to take a leak before we hit the road. As I did, the voice in my head spoke again. "Disgusting. Men are disgusting. I want you to sit and pee from now on, so you don't spatter all over your pants."

"What? I did not spatter. I thought you left." My heart started to race again.

"Now calm down or we're both dead. It always spatters a little. How can it not? It's simple fluid dynamics. My name is Diana, by the way. I'll let you be for a while and we can talk later. We need to resolve this issue. You need to conform."

"Never. Go away."

Zipped up, washed my hands and walked into the corridor. Ellen was waiting patiently by the exit with her suitcase. I picked it up. "All better. Ready?"

"Ready." She kissed me quickly on my lips.

I put her suitcase alongside mine in the front trunk of Arry. Luckily, our suitcases were small.

How the hell was I supposed to handle what just happened? Why was Ellen delivered a box? The boxes had beings that took over people's bodies when they touched the crystal? How can it be? Maybe I was dreaming.

I didn't realize I was staring into the trunk until Ellen tugged my arm. "Looks like we have it all. Ready? You sure you're okay? Want me to drive?"

"Uh, yeah. I mean, I'm okay. I'll drive."

Ralph handed me my key. "Have a good time, sir, and Miss Ellen." He opened her door.

We both slid in and I punched the vacation address from the reservation e-mail on my phone into the GPS. Navigation started and I relaxed some more. Arry calmed me with her attributes and familiar voice as if she were my partner from all the deliveries we made. How could I have done this to all those people? Why didn't they fight it like I am? They all acquiesced immediately.

Ellen started digging through the bags behind the seats. "Oh look. You brought fruit, nuts and jerky. We don't have to stop to eat now. Can I get you something?"

Arry spoke through the speakers, "Right in three-hundred meters and enter the freeway north for three-hundred kilometers."

"Sure, why not. How about some grapes?"

I had to keep it together for Ellen or she'd think I was a lunatic.

"Here you go. Tell me when to stop."

Ellen kept me fed, which kept her busy and allowed me to concentrate. After a few minutes, I saw Ellen yawn as she fed me another grape. "Want to take a nap? You look tired."

"If you're done eating. I didn't get much sleep last night. I was too excited about our weekend."

"I'm done. I could use some thinking time anyway to wrap up my day and put it away for vacation. Lean back and nap."

She kissed me on the cheek as I moved into the middle lane; she leaned back, and closed her eyes.

I had to find a way to get this thing out of me.

The thing spoke inside of my head. "I am not a thing, I am Diana. You can't get me out."

I mentally spoke back to her and tried to stay calm this time. "Your name is Diana?"

"Yes. I told you before."

"Where are you from? What are you? Why are you inside of me? Are there others? Is this what happens when I deliver a box?"

Her pleasant and interesting voice said, "Let me tell you the story."

18

Diana told me her story inside of my head. It was as if she were a lucid hallucination. I felt her emotions like they were my own. She had a lovely voice and her being felt simple and sweet, like Ellen.

"It was when our planet finally died. Our planet was very much like yours, with similar atmosphere and weather, in another dimension. An alternate reality you might say. We had neglected it for so long, it shifted on its axis and the whole population perished - victims of our inability to work together as a planet."

I experienced her grief and could see images of the planet and her loved ones. My eyes began to water. I wiped them.

"Keep right in two-hundred meters," Arry said.

Diana continued, "On our planet, we formed tribes, similar to your own, based on geography, religion, race, and so on. All narcissistic groups, thinking they were right and all others were wrong."

"Diana, tribes? We haven't had tribes for centuries. Maybe some remain in the jungles, but that's all."

"You still have them. You just call them other things. Catholics, Republicans, Democrats, high wage social groups, low wage social groups, and on and on the population slices and dices itself into tribes. See?"

"What's so wrong with that?"

"Nothing, if each tribe didn't think they were the only ones who were right. If individuals would look at things logically, rather than through their blinders of upbringing and tribal beliefs, it would work. However, we didn't manage to. Much as your society is today."

"Okay. I can see that. Like the way my family thinks their beliefs and viewpoints are the only correct ones - their religion, their politics, their beliefs, their food. So you're from another planet, or uh, alternate reality - if everyone died, how are you here?"

"Ekaterina is our gatekeeper. On the planet, she was a very powerful person. Your definitions might call her a scientist and a mystic. She was renowned for her abilities, yet again no one would listen because of their narcissism. She found a way to capture a person's essence and then move it like computer memory by energizing a crystal. The name of the crystal on this planet is phenacite. A somewhat less available crystal, nonetheless, an available, clear, programmable, crystal."

"Is that what I delivered?"

"Yes. When it was inevitable your planet would perish, Ekaterina became your Noah. Except, rather than gathering a diversity of creatures, she gathered like-minded beings from only one tribe - hers. All of us are very similar to your reality's people, except more highly developed. She and Argus set about teaching all of us about your earth and put together a plan to save your planet and many of our beings.

"Before our planet perished, she captured their essences in a computer of sorts, I think you'd call it a quantum computer, and that computer was the ark. She and Argus escaped with many beings' essences retained on that computer and arrived here a year ago. Argus transfers the beings from the quantum computer to the Phenacite crystal."

"Argus?"

"Yes. He was her husband and equally astute. I believe he was the one who was meant to take over your body, not me."

"I see. Why hasn't he?"

101

"He needs to finish the process of loading the crystals with beings' essences. You needed to gain greater wealth to put him in a reasonable position of power when it's time for him to enter you."

"Now it's starting to make sense. Why me?"

"You happen to look much like Argus did. Ekaterina found likenesses of each being's essence for them to enter, so the transition would be the least unpleasant for us."

"Why does everyone just acquiesce so easily?"

"The people chosen as the hosts also needed to have the attribute of being able to conform. She thought you would do so after she tested you a little, though initially you were high risk. It appears you were still high risk, and in Ekaterina's desire to have Argus using you, we now know she would have failed."

"Who are you supposed to be with?"

"Henkle Schlygel was my mate." I sensed her love for him as she saw him in her mind, or, my mind's eye, that is. He did look just like the one I met.

She continued, "Ellen and Henkle were to be together with Ellen as my host. She looks remarkably similar to me as well. There are only so many variations of people. I'm sure you've been mistaken, or likened to someone else."

"Yes, John Candy. Except not anymore because I've lost weight."

"Okay, then you see. There are certainly others who look very similar to you as well."

"So, let's see. How does a person from your planet or alternate reality, get put into the quantum computer? If we know that, maybe we can remove you from me."

I endured her feeling of heartbreak and saw the image of Henkle Schlygel sitting in a high-tech looking chair with electrodes on his head and arms as Ekaterina stood at a hologram panel and waved her hands in front of it. She looked at Diana. "Ready?" Diana started to cry and her pain became mine. Ekaterina tapped the hologram and Henkle Schlygel slumped in the chair, his body dead.

Diana's voice in my head, broken and choppy said, "That's how it works. He's back now, though, in his new host."

"So they could get you out of me then."

"I don't know. She and Argus have only gone in one direction with your particular breed so far. When two beings occupy the same body, it may destroy them both, or remove them both, leaving the host without a driver, no spirit inside and quite dead like we were when our essence was removed and transported here."

"I see."

Diana was silent for a time. I looked over at Ellen sleeping peacefully. "What now?"

Diana turned my head to look back at Ellen briefly. She took my left hand and ran it through my hair, then said to me, "You love each other. I love Henkle. Ekaterina loves Argus. It's such a mess. It would have been so easy if you hadn't interfered. You'd have ended up one of the most powerful men on the planet. The world would be one set of unified beliefs and the non-host humans would follow us like the lemmings they are. Earth would survive. We would survive. You've ruined it all."

"I'd be stuck riding backseat to Argus, and Ellen and I would be apart. I'd be stuck with Ekaterina."

"Would that be so bad, David? Come now. You must have been intrigued by her."

"She's my boss. She's too scary for me. I love Ellen."

"You'd have her if you could, and you know it. You'd acquiesce immediately and follow Argus just to experience their life, and your new life, together."

"I doubt it. I'd be forever in the backseat of the car."

"A quite comfortable car, nonetheless. From the newly introduced DNA, you would survive over three hundred years in perfect health. I don't doubt you would have jumped at it. When the others felt the presence of the new occupant, they all acquiesced from the relief it brought them, and hopped on the bus like good conformists do. You would have as well."

"Maybe. I have the new DNA now? With you in me I'll live three hundred years?"

"Yes. I need to think." Diana said. "I'm not quite sure what to do with our situation."

"Good. I need to think, too. Three hundred years."

19

We arrived at our mountain retreat with no more interruptions from Diana. I almost thought she was a hallucination, I felt so normal again.

When I parked the car, Ellen stretched and yawned. "Did I sleep all the way? Are we there?"

"Yes, we are. The Lodge and Cabins of Mountain Side Resort."

Ellen looked around. "It's beautiful. I never spent any time in the country. I was always afraid of it after living in the city all my life. Spiders and such, you know."

"I'm a city dweller, too, so this will be new to both of us. We need to check in and get our cabin. C'mon."

We climbed the fieldstone steps to the huge, roughhewn-oak, double-door entrance. I pulled the heavy door open and held it for Ellen. We walked to the main desk in the lobby.

"Good evening, folks. You've arrived just in time to view the sunset from your cabin porch. You must be Mr. and Mrs. David Lionetti. You're the last to be checking in tonight," said the man, who wore what looked like a park ranger outfit.

I took my wallet out. "Yes, Lionetti, David and Ellen."

Ellen held my bicep with both hands and smiled up at the attendant. "Hi."

"Hello, Mrs. Lionetti. Would you like to choose the cabin? We have two available, both ready and facing the sunset." He put two laminated pictures, one of each interior before us. One was in dark tones and very woodsy and manly and the other was in pinks and pale blues with lace and bright upholstery and wall coverings. Ellen started to point to the manly looking one and my hand involuntarily reached and pointed to the more feminine one.

Ellen looked at me. "I thought you'd like the other, but I love that one."

The attendant slid a key across the desk with the number eleven on it. "Very well. Lovely cabin. Sign here, sir." He slid a sheet across the counter for me to sign.

I signed it and took the key. "Thanks. Is it up the drive?"

"Yes, just after the last switchback. It's the uppermost cabin on the ridge away from the others. You'll see a sign on it that says, 'Pink Lace Retreat'."

"Thanks."

Nice. I come to the country and get stuck in a pink lace cottage. Diana must have had a part in this the way my hand leapt to that page.

"I did. Get used to it," she said in my head.

Back in the car, we started the drive up the switchback road to the top. Ellen had her window down and her head out - like a puppy, the wind blowing her hair back. "It smells so good out here. Mmm."

Tall pines lined the road with a steep drop on one side and a steep rise on the other. The sun was just beginning to set and we could see the sky taking on a tint of pink away from the mountain.

"This is nice," Diana said.

"Don't start. Go to sleep. This is our vacation." I replied mentally.

We wound our way higher until we reached our cabin at the end of the road. It was a log home, two stories high, swing on the porch, and a very obnoxious pink sign hanging above the stairs with, 'Pink Lace Retreat' and the number 11 below it.

I pulled up to the stairs and we took our things out of the car. When I opened the door, I was shocked at the degree of frilly and lace things. It was like a bad dream. Ellen dropped her bag and threw her arms up. "Yeah! This is so pretty! I love it!"

I heard Diana say, "Perfect. So cute."

I picked up our things and started to go upstairs. "Great. Lovely decor. I feel like I'm in a doll house."

"You picked it, didn't you? We can go back."

"No, no, only kidding."

I put the suitcases on the pink flowered bedspread and opened mine. I unpacked, putting my clothes into the disgusting white and pink dresser and closet with pink padded hangers. "Not disgusting. Pretty," I heard.

Ellen came up the stairs. "It's wonderful. Thank you." She came over to the bed, stood on her toes and gave me a hug. When she moved to kiss me, I pulled away. "No kissing. That's my body," Diana said.

"What's the matter? I thought this would be our weekend to discover each other. Why did you pull away?"

"Uh, I don't know. I think I just need a manhattan and some food."

"Good idea. Let me unpack and we'll go."

"Okay. I'm gonna sit outside and watch the sunset. Hurry up so you can see it, too."

I stopped in the downstairs 'Powder Room', as it was so appropriately labeled, lifted the seat on the toilet, put the seat back down, dropped my pants, sat and peed. "Diana!" I yelled in my mind. "Leave me be."

"It's disgusting to pee standing."

"I don't care what you think. You're supposed to be in the backseat."

"No, as a matter of fact, you are."

"Well, I can't imagine what the other people's lives are like with you aliens in them."

"They're fine. They've conformed."

"Why don't you try it and see what it's like? Leave us alone. I bet you won't make it through dinner without intervening."

"You don't know how good it feels to be in a body again. Even if it is your male one. That pee felt so good."

"Try being in the backseat and see if it seems morally correct to take over, conformist or not."

"David. It's a well-known fact that once someone conforms, whether to religious beliefs or social norms and so on, they give up choosing alternatives. People do it for the comfort of not having to think or make decisions. It's a form of autopilot."

"Good. You do it and see how comfortable it is. Give me my body back."

"You'll see. This will be easy for me. I was a good conformist."

I pulled up my pants, washed my hands with the pink, flower-shaped soap, and dried them on the lace and velvet towel. Yuck.

The sunset was gorgeous and ranged in hue from pink to purple. As I sat on the porch swing, and as long as I didn't look at the pink floral seat pads, it felt like a nice country retreat.

The wooden screen door slammed and bounced. Ellen seated herself beside me in a short, flowery sundress and white heels, her brown hair draped over her shoulders with a silk rose in it. Lovely. She smelled like the country air. "You look wonderful. Should I change for dinner, too?"

She held my bicep in both her hands as she gazed at me. "No. You look wonderful in your black jeans and white button down shirt." She opened one more button, revealing my chest hair. She rubbed it. "I never realized you were so hairy."

"I'm Italian, remember? Like a bear. Wait until you see the rest."

She stared out at the horizon. "Beautiful. Look." She pointed. "What's that?"

A large bird, very large in fact, was circling above the ridge. He had a white head. "Bald Eagle. Wow. It must fish in the lake in the valley. I'll bet he has a nest up here."

"David, do you think, well, I'm making a lot of assumptions here, but do you think someday, if we work out, we could get a place like this? Something in the country?"

"Uh, I guess. I'm accumulating cash pretty quickly. But I don't know how long this job will last. Maybe not long at all. I can sell the car, though, and with the money I have and my other house... we could get something nice and maybe I could sell real estate for a living out here."

She kissed my cheek. "I'd love that. Hungry? I am."

We drove back to the lodge and requested a table by the window. The table was already set for dinner with a cloth tablecloth and matching napkins folded like lilies in the goblets. It overlooked a small pond with a lighted fountain. The outside deck had string lights and a gas fire-pit burning with padded wicker chairs encircling it.

The waiter approached with a linen napkin draped over his forearm. He looked a little unusual. High arched eyebrows, clean-shaven, handsome with his blond hair slicked back wearing a black tuxedo. "Good evening. My name is William and I will be taking care of your every desire this evening. Can I get a cocktail for either of you? Or maybe some champagne or wine?"

Ellen looked at me as she held my hand.

I said, "Can I see the wine list?"

I knew what I wanted. I wanted my Blanton's manhattan. Instead, I said, "I'll take a Sauvignon Blanc from Marlborough, New Zealand, if you have that." Damn it!

"Diana!" I said in my head.

"Oh hush. You were right. I couldn't wait in the backseat and pass this up."

Ellen squeezed my hand. "How did you know? Shall we get a bottle?"

"Yes. A bottle of that and a Blanton manhattan, rocks please."

"Of course, sir."

Diana said, "I hate bourbon."

"You'll get to like it or leave."

"Yuck."

"Quiet."

I said to Ellen. "Interesting. His name is William just like at the Hammer."

"He even acts like him a little. I wonder if he's as gossipy. I knew you were a special agent after the first time you were there. William told me. I didn't believe it at first, though, until I overheard you and Judge Seymour talking."

Ellen was looking around the room. A small gas fire burned in the fireplace. The air conditioning smelled as fresh as the outdoors. Oriental rugs covered the marble floor beneath each table. Rich mahogany crown molding complemented the browns and golds in the woodland wallpaper. "This is a beautiful lodge, David. I'll bet the food is fabulous. What are we going to do for the next three days?"

"I'm not sure. Two city kids in the country. The website said they had tennis, golf, hiking, swimming, fishing, boating, horseback riding, and plenty of places to lounge and read a book. Reading a book sounds good."

"I didn't bring one, did you?"

"No. They have stores in town, though." Diana's presence came forward again and I tried to push her back, but lost. "We could go shopping tomorrow in town!" Damn. Diana made me say that.

"You'd go shopping with me? I'd love that. We could get you some new clothes."

"I don't need any new clothes. We could shop for you."

"Either way. I bet the town is quaint."

Great. I'm going shopping with two women tomorrow. I couldn't wait to see the clothes I'd buy. Of course, that's a small problem next to having to figure out what to do with Diana and the world being taken over by alternative reality aliens.

William appeared with our wine cart. He placed a drink in front of me. "Blanton manhattan sir."

"Thank you." I sipped it - a bit sweet with citrus and oak. Creamy vanilla aroma with hints of nuts, caramel, orange and light chocolate. Delicious. "Awful!" Diana yelled in my head.

"Quiet," I said out loud.

"Excuse me?" William said.

"Sorry. Talking to myself. The Blanton's makes me feel quiet and peaceful."

"Yes it does," he said as he uncorked the wine. He handed me the glass to taste. I passed it to Ellen. She swirled it, looked through the glass at the light, sniffed it and tasted, then swished it in her mouth. "Mmm, fragrant and luscious."

William nodded and completed his pour for her, then poured a glass for me and left the bottle in an ice bucket on the cart. I grabbed the wine quickly and smelled it, held my pinky out and tasted it and knew immediately it was too sweet and flowery for me. Diana commented, "Mmm, Ellen is right."

I washed it down with my manhattan. "Damn you!" Diana said. "Couldn't you let me enjoy it a while?"

My hand moved by no accord of mine and drank water with my pinky finger out, swished it in my mouth, and sipped the wine. I tried to pick up the manhattan. My other hand held my wrist down.

"David, what are you doing?" Ellen sipped her wine, one eyebrow raised.

"Uh, can't decide which I like better." I took my hands off the table and put them in my lap. Diana tried to have me reach for the wine again. I had to stop this. I yelled inside my head. "If you don't stop this, I'm taking you home."

"David, please cooperate. We share, okay?"

"Just let me decide when."

"Fine."

Ellen was looking at me strangely again. "Why are you making those faces and looking around?"

"Just thinking. Sorry. I have to let go of work."

"Yes, you do. Now look at me and let's have our vacation."

The rest of our dinner moved along fairly well, as long as I followed my drink with a sip of water in a reasonable amount of time, and sipped some wine. Of course, I ate some things I normally wouldn't, like escargot, which wasn't bad once I stopped looking at them since I loved garlic. Maine lobster, fortunately all picked out of the gross creature's shell already, followed by a pink cherry mousse for desert. Diana had introduced me to some new foods, yet she remained a pain in the ass.

We drove back to the cabin, how I'm not sure. I drank enough manhattans to be drunk and enough wine to be drunk. Could an additional consciousness handle twice as much alcohol? It didn't seem to be the case.

I pulled the pink lace bedspread back to pink satin sheets and nearly puked on it. I stripped naked, fell into bed, and passed out.

20

I woke up startled and yelled, "Ouch!" I was standing in the bathroom. My stomach felt on fire. A roll of duct tape was on the countertop. I looked at myself in the mirror and wondered if this was a nightmare.

My eyebrows were tweezed to a thin line and trimmed short, my chest had two bald strips and lengths of duct tape were on the counter with what was once my hair. My legs were bald, as were almost everything below the waistline. I heard Diana in my head. "Darn. I thought you were going to sleep through it all. I was almost done. The stomach is the most sensitive, though. I should have known."

"Diana, what are you doing?"

"Your hairy body is disgusting. I'm manscaping you. I found the duct tape in a tool drawer in the kitchen. Let me finish."

"No."

"David, look in the mirror. You can't go out with stripes of hair missing."

"I can't go out with bald legs."

"Yes, you can. You'll see. Let me finish."

I gave control to Diana and she finished while I had cold sweats with each pull and rip then I showered. I wrapped a towel around myself and entered the bedroom. Ellen was dressed in white shorts and sandals with a white lace top. Diana took control of my voice. "You look so cute! I love the top."

"David?"

I took back control. "Yes, lovely."

She looked at my hairless body. "How nice. You manscaped for me." She ran her hand over my smooth chest. "Mmm, you feel so smooth."

"You like it?"

"I love it. When you asked me last night if I wanted you to do that, I said yes, remember? I can't believe you did it all in one day. It must have hurt. You're such a man." She stood on her toes and kissed my cheek.

"Thanks. Anything for you, dear. So was last night fun?"

"Fun? It was incredible. Even though you were a gentleman and we didn't go all the way. You were so tender and considerate. I never had such a thrill, many thrills." Her light green eyes reflected her honesty.

"Good. I loved it, too."

I wished I remembered it.

I thought to Diana, "How did you manage to stay awake?"

"My consciousness was fine. It was your consciousness that sucked the alcohol up. Once you passed out, I had free reign. Ellen is a lovely woman. Such a wonderful body and so sweet and sensual. I wasn't going to allow you two to get intimate, but I couldn't resist."

"Wish I'd had the experience."

"Stick with wine next time and maybe you will."

Ellen said, "Are you hungry? You must be, you drank a lot last night."

"Breakfast would be good."

"You helped me burn a lot of calories last night. So, we eat then shop. I can't wait."

We shopped until we dropped. Diana picked pastel shirts, ties, and golf pants for me. It was enough to make me retch.

The weekend progressed expectedly. It was like having Ellen beside me and inside of me. I couldn't make any mistakes in trying to please her this way, and she loved it.

Vacation ended. Life had to be fixed. The intruders had to be stopped. Too many people had already lost their lives conforming to the wills of these alternative reality intruders. I was the only one who could stop it. But how?

21

Back to work. I had to do everything normally, or Ellen and Ekaterina would know something was up. I was torn about continuing the deliveries, knowing what they did to people, yet I had no choice right then. Diana said I should let Ekaterina know what happened and maybe she and Argus could resolve it. But resolve it to whose satisfaction? Ellen and I would end up having our bodies invaded by Argus and Diana. I knew what had to happen, but I just didn't know how to do it.

I had to get Diana out of me, which had to involve Ekaterina, and then kill her and Argus and put an end to this.

By the end of the day, I was exhausted from my mental stress and listening to Diana. I took solace at the Hammer.

Ellen was at her podium, smiling and happy from the long weekend. "I'm so happy you're wearing your new shirt. I think the pink makes your face looks so rosy."

I kissed her lips lightly. "Thanks, not so sure about the matching handkerchief in the pocket, though."

"It's cute."

"That's the problem."

Diana spoke up, "She's right. Very stylish."

"Quiet." I said out loud.

Ellen tilted her head. "What?"

"I just need some quiet. It's been a tough day."

"Go see William and he'll make you feel better, as usual." She kissed my cheek.

I entered the bar. Stan was in the seat next to mine, hunched over a drink, and running his hand through his thick silver hair. "Hello, Stan."

"David. I was hoping you'd show up. Something awful is happening."

I took my seat.

"Blanton sir?" William said.

"Please."

Stan turned to me. His face looked drawn. He sipped his drink and put it down purposefully. He reached into his coat pocket and handed me a piece of paper. "Read this. It's from Henkle Schlygel."

I unfolded the paper. It was a photocopy of a handwritten note signed by Henkle Schlygel. It said:

'I'm writing this note to prevent any investigation into my death. I am committing suicide because I can no longer live my life as an observer, and have grown tired of trying to gain control. A life lived conforming is not worth living. I hope I'm the only person this has happened to, or our world will soon be in chaos.

Signed, Henkle Schlygel.'

I encountered the pain Diana felt as she howled in grief. My eyes began to water involuntarily. I wiped at them.

"I didn't think you'd take it so hard," Stan said.

"I guess it's just a shock."

"Do you understand anything he wrote? You're the only trustworthy person we know who has spoken to him recently."

I looked at the letter, but had to stop so Diana wouldn't get out of control. "An observer. It sounds like someone was controlling him."

"Yes, but whom? Could it be the mystery woman?"

"I don't see the connection."

"I did some research on her and she died a year ago, after a trip here from Scotland."

"She died?"

Stan sipped his drink and shook his head. "Well, her identity is for a person who has a death certificate. Either she was resurrected or stole this woman's identity, which is what I think happened. So, the mystery woman is even more of a mystery. I thought somehow you might see a connection because you speak with her from time to time and might be aware of her activities."

"I know very little about her."

"There's more. Notes saying things similar to this are showing up across the city. Jack Presser, the man in charge of our transit system, cleaned up a bunch of graft that was going on and then committed suicide, leaving a similar note."

"Jack. Head of the transit system for the city."

"Yes. Do you know him?"

"Uh, no. Never met him."

"It was strange. His secretary said his personality changed completely. He used to be a nervous, fearful, twitchy kind of guy, and one day he received a present from a close personal friend and changed completely. The present was nothing more than a phenacite crystal mounted on a base."

"A present from a close personal friend."

"Yes. And he had no friends anyone was aware of."

"Well, I wish I could help you out. It's tragic."

Stan looked at me and nodded his head. His silver eyes darted around my face as he evaluated my response. He blinked quickly a few times as he looked into my eyes. He put his hand on my shoulder. "I know you're the best at what you do. If there is any way you can help us, let me know. Something's not right."

"Agreed."

Stan waved at William and left the bar.

My drink tasted good. It helped me find a center. Diana was silent. Stan could be getting close to discovering what I did for a living. I could tell he had questions, the way he looked at me before he seemed to put them aside.

"Appetizers, Sir David?"

"No, thank you. I don't have much of an appetite."

"Anything I can assist with? Lady problems?"

"You might say that. Sorry, though, you can't help. I wish you could."

Very good, sir. I'm here if you need me. I'll leave you to your drink so you can contemplate." William moved around the corner of the bar and out of sight.

"Hello, David. Nice pink shirt and hanky," Ekaterina said in my ear.

I looked at her and back at my drink. "What do you want?"

"My, aren't you a bit touchy?" She put her hand on my shoulder and leaned in for a kiss. White leather skirt-suit, high heels, glistening black hair swept around her neck and draped in front of her shoulder. Same exotic eyes.

I brushed her away. "Shouldn't I be? You've ruined my life."

"I've created your life. Which, by the way, is on hold momentarily. No more deliveries for a while. We've run into some complications... a technical issue."

"What's the matter? Taking over someone's body and life isn't as easy as you thought?"

She pulled back, her features turned to shock.

I glared at her. "You look pretty good for a dead person, too."

"David. What are you talking about?"

"You know what. You can drop the ruse. Argus can never take this body over because Diana, who is now mourning Henkle Schlygel, is coexisting in my body right now."

She seemed to be pleased. A flat-lipped smile came across her face. "I wondered if the time ran out on that delivery, or if someone else became the host. That's funny. How does it feel to have a woman inside of you? Are you ready to conform to her?"

I looked around the bar. We were alone. "I never conformed to anything. Why should I now?"

"You seemed to be capable in the beginning."

"As capable as Henkle and Jack Presser and the others? I thought their ability to conform was high. Diana said they would all acquiesce easily. Looks like your plan failed. Quite the rejection rate, wouldn't you say?"

"Yes. We have had a few. Such a shame. Argus will work it out soon. Would you like to remove Diana? We can try."

"Try?"

"Well, yes. We haven't tried taking a consciousness out of a body with two, or even taking one out of your breed."

I needed them to try. But I had to keep Argus out of me afterwards. "Yes. We need to."

"Bring that lovely Ellen of yours along. She belongs to Diana."

Diana spoke to me, "David, no! There is no point of me taking over Ellen without my Henkle. There's no point in living."

"Diana doesn't want Ellen anymore."

"You'll bring her along or there will be no attempt. I'll make arrangements with Argus. It may take some time because he doesn't have a ready interface for a body to a computer, or a computer to a body transfer. He only has the crystal interface right now." She leaned in to kiss my lips. I pushed her back.

"Please. Be civil, dear."

"I'll be civil when we fix the mess you made."

"Oh, grow up."

Ekaterina left the bar. My drink was watery and I had only taken a couple of sips. Diana's grief filled me. William came back. "Let me make you a new drink. That one isn't suitable anymore."

I looked at my watch. Ellen could leave if she wanted to. "No. I think I'll call it a night."

"As you wish. That drink was on the house. I hope you feel better."

"Thank you, William."

Ellen was sitting behind the podium playing with her phone. I kissed her cheek and rubbed her shoulders. She rolled her neck and looked up at me. "That feels nice. Ready to go? I can't wait to see your apartment. I started packing boxes today. We can move me this weekend if you want. We'll need to rent a truck, though."

"Packing? Of course."

"Don't you remember? This weekend? In bed you—"

Diana again. "Of course I remember. Let's go."

"Wait. Let me get my suitcase."

Ellen opened the closet and grabbed her suitcase. I needed to tell her something about all of this. What could I say that she'd believe? She needed to know Ekaterina was a threat to us and not just a nuisance.

Ralph brought the car around while we waited in silence. After we were in the car, Ellen put her hand on mine on the shifter and looked at me, the glow of the instruments on her face. "Is something the matter? You seem awfully quiet."

"Tough day."

"It must be tough being a special agent, always at risk."

"Yes. Risk."

Diana started in, "David. Tell her. Tell her the truth."

"I can't. She won't believe me," I thought back.

All of a sudden, I had no control over my voice and Diana came through. She raised my voice an octave. "Ellen, my name is Diana and I'm in David's body. It was I that made love to you this weekend."

"Oh, David. How silly you are. Are you trying to tell me you're transgender? It's okay if you are."

"Damn it, Diana!" I said out loud.

"David, you seem to be in such conflict. Do you truly think she's a separate part of you?"

"Ellen." I looked at her and back at the road. I started to talk quickly. "Diana is distinct from me. That crystal you received is what I deliver each day. Someone else delivered yours to you. After I'd seen what it did to people, I couldn't let you touch it, and that's why I grabbed it. Little did I know there was another person's consciousness inside of it, and it transferred to me. It's supposed to take over completely, but I don't conform well, and I fought it. That's why I was drinking white wine and manhattans. The wine was for her. That's why my body was de-fured, my eyebrows were manscaped and I have pink shirts and handkerchiefs. She did it all. Nonetheless, her consciousness was meant for you."

I could feel her eyes on me as we drove. She was trying to make sense of it. "Hmm. It's interesting you should think that way."

"The important part of all of this is you need to be wary of Ekaterina, whatever her name is, in case she tries to harm you. That's why she wanted us apart. She wanted my body for a man called Argus to possess. Her lover and mate from an alternate reality."

"David, this is getting very confusing."

We pulled up to the gate of my building. It read the sensor on my visor and slid to the side. We drove to my parking space, I took her suitcase, and we rode the elevator up. I held Ellen's sweating hand.

"Are you okay?" I asked.

"I'm fine. It's you I'm worried about. I think the stress of your job is getting to you. You need a longer vacation."

"I'm not a special agent."

"Yes, you are. You certainly aren't a woman named Diana."

"Thanks. Anyway, what you need to know is that Ekaterina is dangerous. I wish I knew her last name."

"Last Name? It's Macguire. I've seen it on her credit cards."

"Ekaterina Macguire? Russian and Scottish? Explains her accent."

"Sometimes in split nationality homes, they like to use a first name from the mother's heritage with the father's surname."

We arrived at the top floor and the double doors of my apartment were straight ahead. The doors sensed the key in my pocket and the bolt snapped open. I turned the knob and we entered.

"It's beautiful. What a view." She walked to the windows and looked out at the city.

"Come, sit on the couch and we can look out the window."

Ellen cuddled up to me, seemingly disregarding my Diana outburst as stress-related.

"Ekaterina Macguire. Good. Maybe I can track her down."

"That should be easy, as prominent as she is."

"Of course. In any case, I need to kill Ekaterina Macguire and Argus. Hopefully I find them together so I can get them both at once."

"Kill them?"

"Yes. I don't know any other way, or they'll essentially kill us both."

"David, this is serious. Is there something you're not telling me that would help it make more sense? It must be the secrets you need to keep for your assignment."

"Yes. That's it."

"Well you should've just told me that.

"I'm sorry. You're right. Anyway, you'll need to accompany me to the meeting when it's set up. Ekaterina won't allow me to go without you for some reason."

"That's exciting David. I can't wait."

"Aren't you scared what will happen?"

"Why should I be? I'm with the best special agent there is."

Ellen put her head on my shoulder.

Diana spoke to me. "You can't kill them. It wouldn't be right. I don't care about getting me out of your body and into the void, or wherever I end up. Without Henkle, I'm lost. We were together for over two hundred years."

I said out loud, "I have to kill them. For the sake of those they are killing and to protect me and Ellen. They're thieves and murderers in my book."

22

The next morning, I put on some jeans and a button down shirt and made breakfast for us. Ellen came out droopy eyed and grinning. "Morning." She wrapped her arms around me.

"You can't go to work today. I'm off and I want you in my sight at all times."

"Okay."

My phone rang. I took it from the holster on my belt. "Hello."

"Meet me at Mom's house for dinner tonight. I'll tell her we're coming. We need to talk."

"John? What are you talking about?"

"I know what's going on and I already set a plan in motion. We can talk tonight."

"No tell me. What are you up to?"

"Tonight."

He hung up.

Ellen looked at me. "Was that your brother?"

"Yeah. We're having dinner at Mom's tonight."

"I hope she has something other than pasta. It took me two days to get my energy back after that, not to mention I gained three pounds."

"I know."

My God. How did my brother get involved?

I looked around the apartment. A picture was tilted on the great room wall. I walked over to it and felt around the frame. There was a small black box with a six-inch or so wire dangling from it. Someone bugged my apartment. Was it my brother, something to do with Judge Seymour, or was it Ekaterina? I slipped it back where it was.

"Let's eat and go for a ride. We need to kill time."

We spent the day going to museums and aimlessly driving. It wasn't the best diversion for me, since I couldn't stop thinking about it and I wasn't the best company. Diana was somewhat entertained, but being reminded she was there only made things worse. Ellen was oblivious to any problem. We pulled behind my brother's car in my parent's driveway again.

My dad was sitting on a vinyl-covered pillow, weeding in his work clothes, with his tie loosened. He looked relaxed after his day of buying construction supplies for a warehouse that served the trades in the city.

He looked up as we approached. "Hey! It's my Davey!" He dug a weed with his screwdriver and put it in a bucket. "Damn weeds. How do they get here? You know, I think it must be from bird shit. There should be a law against birds shitting. I see you brought your lovely woman. Welcome again, Ellen." He grunted as he slid his legs out from under himself and stood.

"Yeah, Dad, we should start a petition against birds shitting." I gave him a hug and he patted my back.

He whispered in my ear, "Johnny told me. I had a few favors coming yet from your grandpa. It's gonna be taken care of."

"What?"

He pulled back. "You know. Not in front of the girl."

Ellen heard him. "What girl? I don't see any girl."

My dad gave her a hug and kissed each cheek. "The pretty girl I'm kissing, of course. C'mon in and have a drink. Sophia should have them ready. I apologize she didn't cook. Said she was busy cleaning today, so she ordered pizza."

We followed him into the house. Mom was running in little steps in high-heels from the kitchen. Her breasts nearly jumped out of her low-cut, flowered dress. Her black hair was pulled back with a flower in it. She had makeup, jewelry and perfume on. She looked darn good for an old lady.

"Davey! Evelyn!" She clicked across the tile entryway, and hugged us both.

"Ellen, Ma, not Evelyn."

"Right. I know that. That's what I said."

"How come you're all dressed up?"

She looked at herself and back at me. "What, this? This is how I always dress for your dad when he comes home from work, now that you kids are gone. Like when we were first married." She winked.

Ellen smiled and poked me in the side.

Mom fluttered her eyelashes like a movie star. "It makes him young again. I have to get the martinis. There's a pitcher chilling in the fridge. Want one?"

"Sure."

"Evelyn?"

"Ellen. Yes, please."

Mom headed to the kitchen.

John came out of the bathroom on the other side of the living room. "You're here. Good. I left the fan on, so don't go in there for a while. Sausage sandwiches for lunch."

He came over with his arms out. He flashed a lewd smile at Ellen and gave her a full contact hug, squeezing her bottom as he did.

"Hey!" She pushed him.

"That's what I like. You're like Betty before we were married. Hot. He turned to me. How's my little brother?"

"I'm good, what are you up to?"

"Not in front of the girl." He looked at Ellen.

Ellen snipped, "Why does everyone keep calling me a girl?"

"Not now, beautiful," John said

I pushed him toward the door and outside. I could hear my mom as she gave the drink to Ellen. "Here ya go, sweetie. Taking care of men is our real job as women, isn't it? I don't follow all that independent woman stuff."

John and I walked to the sidewalk.

"Where are Betty and the kids?" I asked.

"Ah, she dropped them at a friend's and she's at a woman's erotic toy party. Seems I'm not good enough anymore. She said it will make things more interesting and all her friends are doing it. Go figure. She has a guy like me and you think she'd feel lucky."

"Don't worry about it. It'll work out."

"I know," he said.

He patted my back and stood proudly with his belly out as he rubbed it and looked at me. "I knew you were into something. Good thing you have a brother like me to watch your back. When I heard you say you needed to kill Ekaterina Macguire and Argus, or she would kill you both, I took care of it for you. The hit is set up. They'll be a part of the new skating rink's foundation."

"Johnny, no. Did you bug my apartment?"

"Bug? No bugs there. I sent an exterminator to get rid of them. How do you think they got there?"

"Nice. Putting your brother under surveillance. So do you think I'm a drug dealer?"

"I can't say for sure, but if people want to kill you, you're into something."

"Well you have to stop the hit. You heard wrong."

"I didn't hear wrong. You were clear as day. They already know where she lives and a warehouse she has in her name. Once they get them together. Poof. Problem gone. They'll probably do the hit at the warehouse because it's more private."

"You have to stop it John."

Diana piped up in my head. "He has to."

"I can't. Dad used one of his favors left over from Grandpa and I put it in gear. We aren't allowed to contact them again. Ever. If we do, we die. New way to keep things secure, ya know. Good policy."

I grabbed his shirt collar. "Give me their number."

"It won't do any good. The number is gone already. It's a one time, pay-as-you-go phone they pitch after they get the order. I don't even know their names or where they're from."

"What warehouse?"

"Hell, I don't know. They do, though."

I let him go and started to pace. "Fabulous!"

"I did you a favor and I'm not even asking for one back. You know what it costs to bug a place? Ain't cheap, bro. You should be thankful I got your back."

I stopped and looked at Johnny. He was being a real brother. He did it because he loved me and was protecting me. Diana said, "You're right, David. He loves you."

I choked up and gave him a hug. "Maybe it'll all work out anyway. Thanks for taking care of your little brother."

He pulled me to him and kissed each cheek, then pulled my cheeks with his hand. "Baby Davey." He patted my cheek lightly. "Let's have a martini and some pizza and get out of here so Dad and Mom can relax See how she dressed tonight? The old man has it pretty good."

"Yeah."

I needed to get out of there quickly and warn Ekaterina or I'd be stuck with Diana in me forever. Diana agreed. "Yes, hurry. As much as I like you, Ellen, and your family, I don't think I could live three hundred years like this."

23

Ellen and I didn't eat at my mom's. We said we had a dinner meeting. I called Ekaterina from the car and told her we needed to talk right away. She set up a meeting in a parking lot nearby. I explained to Ellen what was going on, but she still wasn't buying it. If I wanted Ekaterina and Argus dead, why was I trying to save them? When I told her about Diana inside of me again, she just shook her head.

We parked in the back of the lot and waited. Ekaterina pulled in alongside us and we exited the car.

"David. What's so urgent?" Ekaterina stood with us between our cars. She looked concerned as she nervously flipped her long black hair over her shoulder.

"You and Argus have been targeted by mafia hit men."

"Oh, come now. Why would anyone want to do that?"

"Because my brother thought you were going to kill me and he set it up."

"What would make him think that? Does he know what we're doing?"

"No. He thinks you and I are involved in something illegal like drug dealing. Nothing else matters, though. You need to pay attention and protect yourself from the hit men."

Ekaterina looked at me as if I were her best friend. She put her hand on my shoulder. "Thank you. I can't believe you're sincerely trying to save our lives." She kissed my cheek. She walked to her car and popped the trunk. She took out a metal briefcase and handed it to me.

"This is for you. It contains a significant sum of money. I feel I owe it to you."

"So, you're not going to take over our bodies?"

She gave me a stern look. "Argus still hasn't perfected the process. If something goes wrong before we complete our tasks, I want you to have enough money to take care of yourself and Ellen. She was to be the host for my daughter."

"Diana is your daughter?"

"Yes."

"I see. Well, thank you. You should get new identities and go somewhere else." I opened my trunk and put the case inside.

"Yes, but the gateway to the computer Argus is using is limited to one location. It's the only portal to it in this dimension. We need to do our work at the warehouse first."

"So when can I get Diana out of me?"

Ekaterina looked at us both and thought for a moment. "We could go see how he's doing right now and warn him, too."

"Okay, that sounds fine."

"Follow me."

We got in our cars and Ekaterina led the way.

Ellen had questions. "You're still talking about Diana. I thought you made that up to cover your agent secrets. Are you doing that with Ekaterina, too?"

"It's true. There is a person called Diana inside of me. Ekaterina and Argus are from another reality and they plant beings from their world into people here. I know it sounds weird, but you have to believe me."

"Oh, David, never mind. I know. Top secret." Ellen looked out her window as we followed Ekaterina, who raced ahead when we arrived at the long lane of warehouses. I followed slowly, not knowing where the potholes were in the decrepit lot.

Ekaterina's R8, which looked just like mine, was parked by a man door in the back by a dumpster. She had already run inside and we parked next to her. The area was deserted. A potholed lot, rusted metal exterior on the building, and no signage except for "313" above the door. I tested it. It was unlocked. Ellen and I entered cautiously.

Rows of floor-to-ceiling storage racks stretched out before us. It smelled dusty and damp. Most of the racks were empty, except for a few with broken down warehouse equipment on the shelves. We walked to the end where the racks had stacks of wrapping paper, ribbons, and boxes like the ones the crystals were packed in. Across the aisle were phenacite crystals already mounted on bases.

There was an office, where Ekaterina and Argus were talking loudly at the end, yet I couldn't make out what they were saying. We entered and they stopped arguing.

"You're here," Ekaterina said as I closed the door behind us. Argus's face filled with anger. His tall thin frame was rigid as he fidgeted with a pen in his hand. He glanced at us through his thick glasses and then back at Ekaterina. "They shouldn't be here."

"Oh, Argus, it's too late for that. They know all about what we're doing and we have to get Diana out of David's body."

"Why? So, I can take it over? I don't need it. You're jeopardizing our whole plan here. He could be lying about mafia hit men just to get here."

"Argus, my daughter is inside him."

I heard Diana. "She is my mother."

I told Argus, "I'm not lying. You have to watch out. They could show up here or anywhere, and kill you both."

He came closer in his lab coat and peered at me. "We have miraculous healing powers. The only way we die is if we starve to death, like everyone else on our earth did."

He circled me, looking me up and down. "You do have a decent body. The body I have right now is somewhat less desirable and needs supplemental vision aids. However, I have not removed a second consciousness and replaced it successfully yet. I do have the programming done and, if you wait a while, I only need to do a couple more tests.

Ekaterina pulled seats out for us from the table in the corner. "Have a seat."

She stood in her white lab coat, black jeans, and white blouse next to the table. We took the seats.

"I don't understand the coats. I don't see a lab or equipment," I said.

"That's because it's invisible until we make it visible. It resides on another dimension. This location is the portal to it. It controls all the implants. Without it we wouldn't exist."

Argus pulled a chair over from the table to the center of the room, placing it over an "X" on the floor. "Get me another test element, Ekaterina, and quit telling them how this works."

She exited through a door in the back of the office and reentered with a man dressed in ragged clothes with unkempt hair and the stench of a dumpster. His mouth was duct taped shut. Foggy eyes, wide, and full of fear. Yet, he didn't seem to have the strength to struggle. She seated him in the chair and Argus promptly duct taped his legs and hands to the chair.

"What are you doing?" Ellen asked.

Argus replied, "We have to test the program for insertion and removal. He's already had a second consciousness inserted. Now we need to try to remove it."

Ellen whispered in my ear. "What you told me is true? You do have Diana inside of you?"

"Yes."

Argus positioned himself carefully. He raised his hands until they were face-level and a holographic panel appeared. I heard Diana in my head. "David, it's just like the one they used to remove us before. I have to pay attention."

I watched closely as Argus manipulated a series of objects labeled in a way I didn't understand. Some letters were similar, others different. Nothing seemed to make a familiar word. I thought, "Diana, do you understand what he's doing?"

"Yes."

Argus made one last motion, stopped working on the panel and watched the subject. The test subject's eyes rolled back. He shook his head around and tried to scream though the tape. His body tensed. His eyes shot open wide and he stared right at me. He crumpled in his seat.

Argus kicked the chair. "Damn." He cut the tape off the chair with a pocketknife and dragged the body to the other corner of the room.

"Ekaterina, what are you waiting for? Get me another."

"What happened?" I asked.

"You aren't too bright are you? He's dead. I ended up taking both out. Don't worry. They're stored in the computer. Now, I have my planet's test specimen's consciousness and your planet's homeless test specimen's consciousness as well. I only have a few more variables to eliminate and it should work."

This time, Ekaterina brought in a woman about twenty-five years old dressed like a prostitute. She was gagged like the homeless guy. Ekaterina seated her and taped her hands behind the chair while Argus fastened her ankles. The woman didn't seem to be all there.

"Does she know what's happening?" I asked.

Argus said, "She's befuddled because her consciousness is inside battling the other, since like you, they weren't a proper match.

These test subjects are the way they are, homeless, drug addicts, prostitutes and so on, because they didn't know how to conform. In other words, they are very much like you."

"Thanks."

"Okay. I have to watch. Pay attention, David," Diana said inside me.

Argus began again. He moved through his procedure. I heard Diana say, "Yes, that makes sense."

The subject's eyes rolled back in her head, her head rolled on her shoulders. Eyes snapped open. Body tensed and tried to break the bonds and became limp.

Argus kicked the chair and the woman over. Her head made a loud cracking thud against the floor. "Damn it!"

He took his pocketknife and cut the bindings, freeing her body. He dragged her unceremoniously to the corner and stacked her on top of the other body. "I have to remember to erase these trash test subjects from the computer when I finish."

Ekaterina brought in another prostitute. She must have been the dead one's friend. As she came in, she looked at her, dead on top of the homeless man, and started to struggle. Ekaterina and Argus overpowered her thin body and taped her to the chair placed over the "X" once more.

Another series of motions on the holograph from Argus. Another dead subject added to the pile.

The next subject came in talking. He seemed about thirty years old with a short haircut and neatly shaven face. He wore khaki pants and a pistachio-colored golf shirt. "I'm fine, Ekaterina. This host is completely subservient. A perfect coupling. I don't need to be removed from it."

"Nonetheless, we need to test this and see that it works. Don't you want to help save our people?"

She seated him and he looked up at her. "Of course I do."

"Good. Sit there," she said to him.

He sat patiently and watched as Argus made his motions on the holograph. His eyes rolled back in his head. His head rolled on his shoulders and stopped. His body tensed, eyes opened wide and he took on a relaxed look. He looked around the room trying to get his bearings.

Argus smiled and made a few more motions at the holograph while we all watched. The test subject looked at his clothes and hands. "What happened? Is this what happens when you die?" He looked at the bodies on the pile. "That's my body. How did I get inside of this one? This is a guy's body and I'm a not a guy. How am I supposed to make a living servicing men like this?"

Argus laughed. "Patience, young lady. Stay still."

He waved again at the screen. The test subject tensed then collapsed off the chair onto the floor in a heap.

Argus raised his arms in victory. "Did it! Ours out, trash in, trash out. All ready." He wrote something down on a pad and handed it to Ekaterina. "Here's the sequence and the manner to use. Just don't take out the last consciousness like I did."

Ekaterina looked at it and placed it on the table. She gave Argus a hug.

There were a series of loud bangs and the glass of the office window exploded. I pulled Ellen under the table with me as she screamed. Argus and Ekaterina's bodies bled on the floor.

The door opened slowly and large shoes crushed the glass beneath them. Two men entered and stood beside their victims. A masked man looked under the table at us. "Are you two okay?"

"Yes," I choked out.

"Good. Get out of here quick."

24

We returned to my apartment and tried to calm down. Ellen and I weren't used to seeing such violence.

Ellen shakily poured us bourbons from the Blanton's bottle I kept on a table with glasses by the window overlooking the city.

"You don't drink bourbon," I said to her.

"Tonight I do."

We sipped as we looked at each other. She made a face after hers. I heard Diana's revulsion followed by, "Please David, that's horrible. I just saw my mother killed. Have some empathy."

I spoke out loud. "Sorry to cause you discomfort, Diana, but I'm having a strong drink."

Ellen choked a little. "David, stop with the Diana thing."

"You saw what they did. You know it's true."

"I did. Still, you don't have to act like it. I'm not sure I can manage the truth. I don't know how you can do your job as an agent. This is all too strange for me."

"We'll get this fixed somehow." I held her chin and kissed her lips.

Using my voice, Diana said, "We have to get back into the warehouse and I can remove myself. I don't even care where I end up."

Ellen looked at me. I shrugged my shoulders. "Sorry. She's having a tough time."

Ellen walked over to the windows to look at the city.

"Is there a way to destroy the computer?" I asked Diana.

Diana and I conversed in my head. "That can't happen. It would release all the beings' essences to nothingness and all the hosts would lose the inhabitants they had to the void. It would be the annihilation of my species."

"And then what?"

"I don't know. Your world would suffer as well. We would never get to clean it up and save it from self-destruction. This reality of yours would ultimately die as well."

"Would that be worse than having people riding in the back seats of their bodies?"

"It wouldn't have been a problem if they conformed and acquiesced to us."

"We both know that doesn't always work. Would you want to be me right now, having you in my body? Is that something you'd want done to you if our situations were reversed? Come now."

Diana became silent. Ellen walked back to me. "What about the briefcase? Should we look inside, or do you think it could be a bomb or something?"

I walked over to the table and ran my hands across the cool metal exterior of it. "I don't think it's a bomb. Ekaterina wouldn't destroy her daughter."

"Then open it. Maybe we can just disappear if it's enough." Ellen ran her hands over the case. She finished her drink, put it on the table, and looked up at me.

I ran my thumbs over the latches. There were combination locks on each of them and they were set on all ones - eleven eleven. I tried the latches. They flipped open. I lifted the lid.

I couldn't believe what I saw. The case held stacks of hundred dollar bills, gold coins in clear tubes, what appeared to be cut diamonds in other clear tubes, and multiple passports from English-speaking countries with no pictures yet.

Ellen began picking up the contents as I did. We were mesmerized. "How much do you think this is?" she asked.

"I'm not sure. It's a lot." The diamonds alone would be worth a fortune.

Relief came with the financial security it brought and I got myself another drink.

Ellen joined me as I looked out at the city. As I stood under the spotlight shining down in front of the window, Ellen grabbed the shoulder of my shirt. "You have blood on your clothes."

I looked at it. Diana choked up, as did I, when she said, "My mother's blood." Her mother - someone so riveting, I would get lost in her whenever she tried to speak to me. I wiped a tear from my eye.

I looked at Ellen's clothes. She had splatters as well. "We'll need to get rid of these. We wouldn't want to be tied to the murders somehow."

"I'm sure your agents will clean it up."

"I'm not a secret agent. I deliver the boxes."

"Whatever you say David. Are we taking tomorrow off? Why don't we just use the passports and go away?"

"I have to get Diana out of me. After that, we can do what you want."

Diana said, "Thank you, David."

25

We slept a bourbon sleep. I woke before Ellen, showered, and made a pot of coffee. The balcony of my apartment had a constant breeze, which seemed to wash away my trepidation about thinking through what to do next.

I could take the passports and money and disappear, but I still wouldn't be free of Diana. Diana suggested going to the warehouse, so she could attempt to remove herself from me. I wasn't certain it wouldn't be a crime scene, not to mention the risk of it was high. I put on the news, slumped on the couch, stared at the TV, and ate cookies.

Ellen came out with a glass of milk and joined me. When the hour struck, another program came on and the headline story was, "Four found dead in a dumpster in the warehouse district. Identities unknown at this point." But with Ekaterina and Argus, there should have been six - four test subjects and them.

I guess my brother was wrong about them ending up in the cement of a skating rink, if it was them. The reporter said a homeless person found them this morning while looking for breakfast.

My doorbell rang. I turned down the TV and answered it.

"Sir David." William stood smiling in a three piece, pinstriped, charcoal business suit. He certainly didn't look like a bartender.

"What are you doing here? How did you know where I lived?"

"I came to pay you a visit. We need to talk."

"Well, come in."

He stepped through the doorway and promptly smiled and waved at Ellen. "Good morning, Lady Ellen."

"Good morning, William," Ellen chimed.

I showed him a seat. "Take a seat and let me get YOU something to drink for a change. Coffee? Juice?"

"No, thank you, sir." He seated himself at the dining room table. "I've just had breakfast and I'm quite satisfied in all respects."

I seated myself adjacent to him. "So, how can I help you?"

He leaned toward me - his face full of concern. "Have you seen the news yet?"

"I saw some of it, yes."

"The piece about the four bodies placed in the dumpster?"

"Yes. Why do you ask?"

"Well, you see, last night I tried to reach some people who work for me, but couldn't. I still haven't reached them and I thought you might be able to assist. With your background, that is."

"I see. Why would I be able to assist and who are these people? I didn't know you had anyone working for you."

"You see, I am not the person you think I am. You had an association with one of my people that may help shed some light on what may have happened to them."

"William. I never was a secret agent of any sort."

"Of course, sir. I always knew that."

"Then why did you tell others I was?"

"I had to build you up and make you seem valuable, or people would suspect where all your wealth came from. You are a part of my team. Let me continue, it will become clearer to you. The one person I am currently interested in hearing about, is Ekaterina Macguire. The mystery woman."

William sat back in his seat, rigid and formal as ever, and looked like the perfect gentleman. His smile revealed no malice.

I stared at him. "Ekaterina worked for you?"

"Not in my employ, per se. Though she is one hierarchical level below me, how would you term it, the totem pole, yes."

My mouth hung open. Ellen shut the TV off and came over to sit with us. William nodded to her politely.

I heard Diana in my head. "It's him. He's the one heading it all up. He's our leader and most likely thinks you killed them."

He touched my shoulder. "You seem to be without words. Can you shed some light on what happened to them? I've already replaced them so the deliveries can continue, which means you'll need to get back to work soon. However, there are a few loose ends. When I checked the security cameras, your car and Ekaterina's were seen arriving at the warehouse. The camera feed went black a couple of minutes after that. When I checked the warehouse, a window had been replaced in the office, but everything else seemed okay. Except some blood spatter under the tabletop, which indicates something may have happened to them."

"Uh. We followed Ekaterina to the warehouse, yes. I was warning them of a threat to their lives."

"Ah, yes, you have been such a loyal employee. I'm sure they were thankful."

"Ekaterina was, but Argus was angry we were there."

"I see." He looked blankly at me as if trying to discern my guilt or innocence. "Then what?"

Do I tell him the truth that they were killed by hit men? Do I try to say I know anything? What would he think?

He nodded as if he had found his answer. "I already know. You wouldn't have put the camera feed out after you arrived if you intended to kill them. You would have done it before, so I know you didn't do it. You have revealed your innocence by virtue of the camera feed timing, and my being able to ascertain you aren't their killer. You see, I can read minds as well as Ekaterina - better in all truth. It's not so much them I'm concerned about as it is your loyalty and what to do with you. Now I know you're loyal to our cause and will be able to continue."

I stared blankly at my bartender, world takeover leader. "What if I said I no longer desire to continue deliveries? I'm retiring."

He looked at Ellen. "You love Ellen, do you not?"

"Yes. I do."

He looked back. "It seemed strange your relationship survived the vacation you took, since Diana was already in control of Ellen. Diana is Ekaterina's daughter and not very much akin to the real Ellen's personality, only her looks." He leaned toward Ellen and looked into her light green eyes. "What happened, Diana?"

Diana took over my voice. "I'm in here, damn it. David saved Ellen from the transfer. Ellen is still Ellen."

William formed a grin I hadn't seen on him before, entertained and somewhat evil. "Sir David. My, my, you do seem to have problems with the ladies, now don't you?" He chortled. "How do you like being a nonconformist and not allowing Diana full use of yourself? It must be somewhat disturbing. Might be worse for appearances, though, if she did have full control." He slapped my shoulder.

"We get along okay."

Diana took over my voice. "David is fine, and I need to be removed. This is no life for anyone for three hundred years. You need to remove me from him, William."

I nodded.

"Once we have completed the process we've begun, we will set things right for Ekaterina's daughter."

"She can't have Ellen."

"Well then, we'll have to find another suitable host. It can be done. There are many similar variations on this planet, I'm sure."

"Can we do it now? Do you know how?"

"Of course. The programs are still in the computer Argus set up and we have new operators that are very good at what they do. However, now is not the time. We have work to do. You need to start deliveries again. Then, afterwards, we can talk."

"What about the problems with the transfers? Like Henkle Schlygel, Jack Presser and, uh, myself?"

"Yes, there was some unexpected fallout. Your planet will survive even with the few losses. The fallout was from nonconforming beings, which are entirely unacceptable in order to have a viable and long surviving planet, wouldn't you say, Sir David? Conformance is key in any society, and key to acceptance of our beings."

"I wouldn't know."

"You saw how Henkle helped to clean up the drug problem and gun smuggling and how Presser started to clean up the graft in the transportation system. Other examples are out there as well. You need to watch the news more. You'd see how conformance has been beneficial to the survival of your planet and your species."

"I suppose so. But I don't think globally. I'm pretty much a friend-and-family kind of person."

"David, if we don't complete the mission, all of our remaining beings and your planet will be destroyed. We need to finish this. Diana can then be removed and put into an appropriate body so she can live the life she deserves as well. You and Ellen can then retire and live the life of Riley for all I care. But we must complete the transfers."

I heard Diana in my head. "He's reading your mind again. Careful."

I thought about the planet being saved from our continued assault on it and the way it might be if all this worked. It could be a better place.

"Yes, Sir David. A few losses to save the many. Not unlike your wars. Much less gruesome, though, wouldn't you say?"

"Yes."

"Good." He glanced at his watch. "I have to follow up on the transfer team. You'll be receiving your text messages from another number. Put the number in your phone as something benign when you get it. It will be prefaced with 'Argus', though that was nothing more than a wish of Ekaterina's and there is no point in changing it."

William stood and put his hand out. "I'll see you at the Hammer."

I shook it and nodded.

He turned to Ellen, bowed, and said, "Good day, Lady Ellen."

Within the hour, I received a text.

26

I completed four deliveries. One was to a particularly rich executive who, immediately after touching the crystal, called his secretary in, gave her a raise, and then asked her to find philanthropic ventures for him to get involved in. He said he had made enough off other's misfortunes and it was time to give back.

After I heard that, I thought these beings from an alternate reality might very well be doing the right thing for all of us. Diana supported it as well, even though she was still stuck inside.

I visited the Hammer as if nothing had changed. William was as William had always been. I ordered my drink and some 'sow fromage canapes' as William called them. I promptly dunked my coat sleeve in them getting cheese stuck on it. I was trying to get it off to no avail when Stan showed up.

He took a seat next to me. "Hello."

William came over. "Judge Seymour. The usual, sir?"

"Yes, please," he answered.

Stan turned to me. "I received some information that has me somewhat disturbed. The mystery woman can't be located."

"Is that so?"

"Two prostitutes, a homeless person and a shoe salesman were placed in a dumpster in the warehouse district. When the authorities looked up the owners of the warehouse the dumpster was nearest to, they found she owned it. Investigating, the authorities found the video security system disabled."

My heart started to race. Did he get the video with my car in it. "That's awful. She's dead?" Sweat dripped from my armpits down to my rib cage.

"I never said that." He paused and observed me then began again. "They checked the camera feeds and, unfortunately, there was no recorder and it didn't appear to be a crime scene. The warehouse seemed in order when they investigated. They found an inventory of crystals on bases, similar to the one found with Jack Presser when he wrote that odd suicide note. The one delivered by a close personal friend that seemed to change his personality completely, according to his secretary, after it was delivered. A whole inventory of them. Any idea what Ekaterina may have been doing with them?"

Sweat continued to drip. "No. No idea. Interesting."

"Yes, yet inconclusive." He sipped his drink and looked at me. "Well, the old battle ax should be crying her starvation woes soon, so I may as well head into the restaurant. Enjoy your evening." He patted my shoulder.

"Thanks, Stan."

He left and William came over. I leaned over and whispered, "No recorders."

William whispered back, "No. Fortunately, I removed it before they arrived and cleaned up the remaining blood spatters from the killers as well. Wouldn't want our transfer facility turned into a crime scene would we?" He straightened and smiled. "Appetizers, sir? Did you have a good day?"

"This is a bit unsettling."

"It will work out."

"How did the day go?"

"I was able to see an interesting transformation. Greedy businessman became a philanthropist."

"Very good. See what a rewarding thing you are doing? An absolute service to mankind. A veritable knight in shining armor." He looked toward the lobby and I turned to see what was happening.

A woman was shouting in the lobby. Stan's wife was interrupting him as he spoke to Ellen. "Stop hitting on the girl and let's eat!"

Stan raised his arms as if to fend off her attack. "Yes, dear."

I turned back to William as he was wiping his hands on a napkin and looking over my shoulder smiling and nodding at someone behind me. I smelled Ekaterina's scent. I felt her hand on my shoulder and a pinch in my neck. I tried to turn around to see her.

I heard my mom saying,"*David! You can't stay like this. Come back now!*"

27

I opened my eyes and the light burned as if I were looking into the sun. Tears ran down my cheeks. There were blurred shapes moving around me and there were unintelligible sounds. A soft hand touched mine.

I smelled a familiar scent as I struggled to make sense of what was happening. A pleasant fragrance. A fragrance that made me feel loved.

"Can you hear me? David, thank God. They said you might not make it. It's me, honey. It's your mother."

Struggling to focus, I wiped my eyes and sat up with difficulty.

"Damn. How come I'm so sore?"

"You haven't moved in three weeks." She kissed my forehead.

My dad wrapped his arms around me and gave me a hug. "Thank God. We'll need to put some extra in the basket this Sunday for sure!"

He kissed my cheeks.

I looked around the room. "Ellen, Ekaterina, William. You're all here. Ekaterina, I thought you were dead."

Ekaterina gave me a strange look from her beautiful, exotic face. She was much more casually dressed than I remembered her ever being - a flannel shirt and jeans.

She spoke in her usual enticing accent. "Not dead. We thought you might be, though. So happy you're back."

Confused, I looked at Ellen and asked, "Can you tell me what's going on?" Without waiting for an answer, I looked at William and said, "What's going on, William?"

My mom slapped my arm. "Davey! Respect the priest! It's Father William."

"Okay, mom. So.." I cleared my throat. "Father William, What's going on?"

He spoke in his normal, elegant way. "Sir David. You wouldn't remember, but I gave you your last rites sir. 'May the Lord protect you and lead you to eternal life', and all of that. Thank the Lord, you've made it."

I must have looked panicked, because Ellen came over and took my hand. "It's okay. There will be some memory loss, yet still, you should recover. You seem to have made it past the barrier. The pressure on your brain is gone. I'm your doctor, Ellen Birman."

She read my vital signs from the monitor above the bed. "BP and pulse are normal and brain activity looks normal." She looked at me. "You're going to be fine, congratulations. Being spoken to by your family while in the coma may have helped."

Outside I heard a woman yelling. "Stan! Go quick. He came to! We have to see him so I can get something to eat. I'm starving."

Stan walked in wearing a white uniform with his portly wife beside him. He said, "Look, Dave's awake!" He shook my hand, his silver hair and eyes as I remembered them. "Congratulations, buddy! We've been pulling for ya."

"Judge. What are you doing here?"

"Judge? Wouldn't want that job - too much stress. I'm just the orderly who's been flipping you over and changing your clothes with my wife here."

I stared at all of them in confusion. I looked at Ekaterina. My mom and dad were normal. William had on a priest's suit and collar. They were quiet, watching me closely.

On my nightstand was a phenacite crystal mounted on a base like the ones I delivered. I pointed at it. "Who's crystal is that?" I said.

Doctor Birman said, "That one's mine. I left it by your bed for good luck."

Stan said, "My wife and I have one too. They're so relaxing, aren't they Doctor?"

"I like them," Doctor Birman said.

Stan said, "The wife is hungry so we have to go. Remember Dave, why question something if it's good? Glad to see you're back." They turned and left.

I looked around the room some more. A fancy looking suit hung on the coat rack in the corner. There was cheese stuck on one sleeve and there were expensive Italian loafers under it.

"How did I get here? What happened? The last thing I remember was William getting me a drink at the Velvet Hammer. He was the leader of the alien invasion that Ekaterina had been handling with her husband, Argus, before she was killed."

Ellen, Doctor Birman that is, took my hand and looked me in the eyes. "It's normal to have this kind of reaction after one's been in a coma. Some people dream, some don't. You must have had quite a dream after that hawk knocked the part off the rack in the factory and it hit you in the head."

"Factory? I still work in the factory?"

Ekaterina spoke up. "You did. Not anymore though. Now that we're married, we have more pressing business."

"Married?"

My mom said, "No wedding or anything. You could have told us Davey. Especially when you were dating someone else." She looked at Ellen and shook her head. "Sorry Doctor Birman, you look like someone else. I'm getting old." Mom sighed.

Mom continued, "Ekaterina showed up with Father William one day, after you disappeared for days when you had eloped. I should call Ekaterina, Doctor Macguire in public."

"No need for that, Mom," Ekaterina said.

Mom continued, "Ekaterina and Father William came over and told us you and Ekaterina married, and that's when they told us about your accident and that you were in the hospital. God bless them. I didn't know what upset me more - not being involved in your wedding or the accident. Anyway, They're paying for everything, and any woman that has a priest for a friend, and is a doctor, can marry my son any way she wants want to." Sophia smiled at Ekaterina.

Ekaterina smiled back. "Thanks Mom."

I looked at the two of them and they obviously knew each other and Mom liked her. "So you're a doctor?" I said.

"Don't you remember? I research alternate reality theory." She ran her hand through my matted hair as she gazed at me lovingly.

"You didn't give me an Audi R8?"

"You've driven mine from time to time."

"I don't deliver packages at a thousand dollars a delivery?"

"Don't be silly. Who would pay such money?"

I looked down in thought then noticed my belly. "I'm not fat."

"Absolutely," Dr. Birman said. "And if you can keep it off as you restore muscle mass, you'll be in the best shape you've been in a long time. With some physical therapy and patience, that is."

My mom said, "We'll get you looking good again. Plenty of pasta and bread. Nice and healthy."

I put my hand under my hospital gown and felt my chest. "No hair. Did you use duct tape to get it off?"

Dr. Birman said, "We wouldn't do that. Just a razor. We needed to shave it for the monitors and in case we needed to resuscitate you."

"So, we're not dating and we never vacationed in the country?"

"Of course not. You're married to Ekaterina."

Ekaterina cast me an evil eye. The gorgeous, exotic, doctor and my wife. "You're a doctor who researches alternate reality theory?"

"Yes."

"So, could I have been in an alternate reality and you have been an alien invader there?"

She laughed. "In theory, yes, but listen to yourself."

"Then in another reality could there be a problem left unsolved?"

"There are many problems left unsolved in this reality, and others, I'm sure." She sat on the edge of the bed, took my hand, and smiled. Her eyes enchanted me. "Let's take one step at a time and get you better. We can talk about theories later. You need to conform to your current situation so you can move ahead."

"Conform?"

I didn't like the sound of that. Ekaterina stroked my cheek with her silken, seemingly pore-less skin. I smelled her sweet breath as she leaned in and kissed my forehead and then smiled at me from that exotic high-cheek-boned face with the drawn-back eyeliner around light blue eyes with rings of black. I melted.

"Well, you are a doctor. I'll settle for that answer. So, a hawk knocked a part onto my head and I've dreamt all this stuff. I think an alternate reality has better odds than that."

Ekaterina kissed me again. "You could be right about those odds."

I couldn't help to think I might have been dreaming right then. She was beautiful, intelligent, loved me, and was my wife. Though confused, I felt lucky to be alive and ready to celebrate. All I could think of was having a Pabst and a Big Mac.

I heard a voice in my head. "David, I can't stand beer. A nice white wine would be much nicer and McDonald's is so fattening."

My eyes popped wide open and I looked at Ekaterina. My heart was racing.

She leaned down, stroked my hair, and whispered in my ear, "I heard that. Once you learn to conform like everyone else, life will be easy. Right now, I'll get you a Pabst and McDonald's. Later, we can take care of Diana. Doctor Birman will be a perfect host for her, Argus my love."

I hope you've enjoyed the read. If you have, please leave a review and tell your friends about it.

Thanks,

A.J.

http://www.AjAaronOnline.com

20103157R00099

Made in the USA
Middletown, DE
15 May 2015